High Cheekbones

High Cheekbones

by ERIKA TAMAR

To Joanna Cole,
agent extraordinaire *and friend*

VIKING
Published by the Penguin Group
Viking Penguin, a division of Penguin Books USA Inc.,
40 West 23rd Street, New York, New York 10010, U.S.A.
Penguin Books Ltd, 27 Wrights Lane, London W8 5TZ, England
Penguin Books Australia Ltd, Ringwood, Victoria, Australia
Penguin Books Canada Ltd, 2801 John Street, Markham, Ontario, Canada L3R 1B4
Penguin Books (N.Z.) Ltd 182–190 Wairau Road, Auckland 10, New Zealand

Penguin Books Ltd, Registered Offices: Harmondsworth, Middlesex, England

First published in 1990 by Viking Penguin, a division of Penguin Books USA Inc.
1   3   5   7   9   10   8   6   4   2
Copyright © Erika Tamar, 1990
All rights reserved

LIBRARY OF CONGRESS CATALOGING IN PUBLICATION DATA
Tamar, Erika.   High cheekbones
Erika Tamar.   p.   cm.
Summary: Fourteen-year-old Alice discovers there's a lot more to being a high fashion model
than designer clothes and a glamorous life-style.
ISBN 0-670-82843-2   [1. Models, Fashion—Fiction.]   I. Title.
PZ7.T159Hi   1990   [Fic]—dc20   89-35263

Printed in the United States of America
Set in Electra.

High Cheekbones

1

Alice Lonner and her little brother Jamie walked along First Avenue, heading back toward the Food Emporium on 57th Street, weaving in and out of sidewalk traffic. From a distance, Jamie, at seven, looked like a miniature version of his fourteen-year-old sister. Both were tall for their ages, lanky, bony, dressed in frayed, faded jeans, navy sweatshirts, and dirty, scuffed sneakers. Jamie even moved in conscious imitation of his sister's bravado style. But all resemblance ended with their faces: Alice's was angular with dark brown hair severely pulled back by a rubber band, and Jamie's was round and soft, fine, almost-blond hair falling into his face.

Alice liked to go fast, walking tough, bopping along, but she had to keep slowing down for Jamie. It was a pain. Walking slow made her feel discouraged. Damn it, she wished he didn't need her so much!

"And wipe your nose," she said. "You think anyone's gonna deal with a kid that's got snot hanging off his nose?"

"I don't got a tissue," Jamie said, sniffling.

"And I told you, say 'ma'am.' 'Yes, ma'am,' not 'yeah.' "

"I forgot," Jamie said. "I'm sorry, Alice."

Because if you said "ma'am," they gave bigger tips. Alice didn't care, she could talk phony-polite from now until doomsday and it didn't touch her deep inside place. But this last one, now, had been a real bitch! It was two blocks over, in a walk-up, so they'd carried the grocery bags all the way up the stairs to the third floor. Alice could tell the bag was too heavy for Jamie. And then the lady gave them a quarter each!

Jamie wiped his nose with the back of his hand and left a smear of dirt all over his upper lip. He looked all tired out and he was getting that faraway look in his eyes, like he wanted to cry.

"Okay," Alice said. "We'll take a break before the next one."

They were back in front of the supermarket again. Alice watched a blue-haired old lady wheel out a cart piled high with groceries. People with their own carts never wanted help, anyhow.

Jamie coughed and sniffled.

"Are you cold?" Alice asked.

"No."

"You want to go back home?"

"I'll stay with you," he said.

It wasn't that cold out. It was a late-February thaw. And he was better off outdoors with her than staying home with Claire. Alice only called her Ma during the good times. This week, she was Claire. Claire wasn't all that bad; she'd just get the blues and they had to run their course. She'd sit around all day in her nightgown, doing nothing, looking off into space. She'd been like that all week.

Claire was all right when she wasn't depressed. During her good times, she'd work temporary and make good money—she could type fast as the wind—and she'd look pretty, skinny and made-up with glittering eyes. She'd be too full of energy and she'd talk and talk. And they'd eat take-out Chinese food.

A woman in a fur coat came out through the supermarket's automatic door. Alice glanced at Jamie. He looked tired, but this one was too good to miss.

"Help you with your bags, ma'am?" Alice asked.

The woman walked right by. She could have said, "No, thanks," at least.

Jamie sat down on the sidewalk, leaning against the slate wall just below the large plate-glass window. Alice stood next to him, her foot up on the ledge.

"Hey, kid, you got any spare change?"

Alice looked up, startled. The boy in front of her looked much older, maybe even twenty. "Do I look like I got any spare change?" she said.

He shrugged. Her hand touched the money in her jeans pocket. He kept standing right in front of her.

"You ought to be giving *me* your loose dimes," she said. "You in your Adidas and designer jeans!" She smiled at him in a friendly way and was relieved when he smiled back. After all, he was a hell of a lot bigger!

She watched him operating for a while. Some people

reached into their pockets for him, most didn't. Three people in a row brushed right past without looking.

Then a man in a business suit mumbled, "Sorry. No change," and hurried on by.

"That's okay," the boy called after him. "I'll take a check. You got an honest face."

Alice laughed. She didn't mean to, it just came out, so then the boy drifted over to them and started talking, like they were friends or something.

"That loser wouldn't give nothing to his own grandmother," he said.

And then, a little later, "Poor people give, you know, like they been there. The fur coats, forget it. . . ."

Alice worked just the opposite. She approached the ladies that looked like Sutton Place—furs or soft wool coats in pretty colors, nice shiny shoes. But she and Jamie weren't asking for any handouts. They were different!

She wondered what kind of habit he was supporting. She wished he'd go away and pick some other corner. He kept talking to them, and Alice didn't want people thinking she and Jamie were with him.

One time, she'd caught Claire out on the street with Jamie. That was when he was little, when they were still on welfare. Alice caught Claire telling a story about having lost her subway fare. Alice had grabbed Jamie's hand and pulled him straight home. She had told Claire good, then! Claire wasn't ever going to use Jamie like that, not ever again!

A lady in a tweed suit and leather gloves came out of the store with two bags. She looked good, and anyway, Alice didn't want to stay on the corner anymore.

"Come on, Jamie," she said.

He got to his feet unwillingly.

"Come on. This can be the last one."

One more decent tip and they'd have enough to buy some of that barbecued chicken and Almond Joys, too. When Claire was like this, there was nothing but peanut butter sandwiches for dinner, nights on end. Claire kept saying how nutritious peanut butter was. Alice thought they were all turning yellow from it.

"Help you with your packages, ma'am?"

The lady had dark hair, cut short and curly, and shiny red lipstick. "All right," she said. She handed the smaller bag to Jamie.

"Where to, ma'am?" Alice said.

"Fifty-eighth and Second."

Alice watched Jamie when they crossed First Avenue. He needed both hands for the bag. She watched out for cabs barreling around the corner and tried to guide him across with her body. She hoped the lady hadn't noticed the panhandler waving good-bye to them.

He really did have designer jeans. A little worn, but still, he had some nerve! Alice wanted a pair of Jordaches like Laurie's, in school.

They had walked a little way when Alice had a funny feeling. She glanced at the lady and the lady was staring at her. Their eyes met and the lady looked away quickly.

Then, further up the block, she felt the lady looking at her again. Looking at her strange. Studying her. Oh, hell, Alice thought, I drew some weirdo! The city was full of them. She was always telling Jamie to watch out.

"How old are you?" the lady asked.

"Fourteen."

"Fourteen," the lady repeated.

Well, at least she lived in a good building, doorman and everything. But even if it had been some walk-up, with a dark, dingy hall like theirs, Alice figured she and Jamie could handle it. She wasn't scared or anything, just spooked by the way the lady kept on sneakily studying her.

The doorman opened the door for them and said, "Good afternoon, Miss Richards." So he knew her.

They walked through the long lobby toward the elevators. There was a crystal chandelier and a maroon carpet.

"You have very good bones," the lady said to Alice.

Jamie picked up on that. "Bones?" he said incredulously.

In front of the elevator, the lady handed them each a dollar and took her bags. She didn't stiff them, weird or not.

"Thank you, ma'am," Alice said.

"Thank you, ma'am," Jamie echoed, and they turned to go.

"Wait," the lady called.

"Yes, ma'am?"

"Have you ever thought of modeling?"

"Modeling?"

"You have excellent bones." She fumbled with the grocery bags and pulled a card out of her purse. "Here. Think about it, dear. If you're interested, give me a call."

Alice held the card in her hand and watched the lady disappear behind the closing elevator doors.

"What did she mean?" Jamie asked. "About bones?"

"I don't know." Alice looked at the card. It said Iris Martin

Agency and an address and phone number. In the corner, it said Pat Richards. She ran her finger over it: the lettering stood out from the cardboard. She stuffed it into her jeans pocket.

"Why does she want you to call?" Jamie asked.

"I said I don't know."

"Where're we going now?" He was such a pest, asking and asking things!

"Back to the store. We'll buy some stuff."

"What're we buying?"

"Leave me alone a minute! Let me think!"

Modeling? Probably it was one of those dumb modeling schools that charged a whole lot of money. There had to be some kind of sucker angle. She wasn't going to be like Claire, always getting lost in dreams. "Sweetie, you'll see, when our ship comes in . . ."

She wasn't anything like Claire and she wouldn't ever be, either. She would graduate from Design Trades and get herself a real life. No way was she going to let her mind wander in the clouds.

At the checkout counter, back at the Emporium, Alice deliberately kept her mind blank. But her eyes kept skirting around the covers of the *Seventeens* and *Mademoiselles* on display there and . . . She was nice-looking, she knew that, and . . . No! It could be anything. The lady could be crazy. It could be a porn ring for kids. Anything at all. No sense in thinking about it.

All the way home—carrying the barbecued chicken, pushing Jamie to walk faster, watching out for traffic—all the way home, she had the feeling of that little card in her jeans pocket.

2

"Come on, Jamie!"

"Okay," he said, but he was still dragging along.

Alice sighed with exasperation and slowed her pace to match his. She could smell the barbecue sauce right through the grocery bag and she was going to dig in the minute she got home.

They were walking up First Avenue, past Ali Baba's and then the window with the orange and red miniskirt. Then the shadows of the 59th Street Bridge and the rancid oil smell of the popcorn place and then the bag lady. People rushed by the old woman without looking. Alice didn't want to see her either, but she did, every single time, either here or down on 58th Street, no matter how hard she tried to keep her eyes averted. She was squatting against the building, in the same khaki coat with the hole in the sleeve, with layers of different faded colors and prints peeping out from under the hem, clutching the stuffed Hefty bag to her side, her toes sticking out of her shoes.

"How come she's wearing all those clothes?" Jamie said. "It's not that cold out."

"Because she's crazy," Alice said fiercely. "Plain crazy. Never mind about her."

It was dumb to feel creepy on account of her. There was no way they'd wind up on the street someplace. Even if their building got torn down, Claire would find someplace else for sure. Anyway, it wouldn't get torn down for a good long time. The one next door, a twin to Alice's, had been boarded up forever and they still hadn't got around to it.

Alice glanced up at it as they passed. Claire said the rats would come out of there when it got demolished. Well, that didn't mean the rats would have to come next door to their apartment. If they were smart, they'd make tracks down the block to that big white high-rise with the awning. Alice could picture the doorman going nuts as they paraded in right through the lobby.

When Alice first got friendly with Rosie in school and told her she lived on East 60th, Rosie had said, "What's a rich kid like you doing in vocational school?"

Alice had laughed. Their block was all mixed up—that high-rise, a swank antique shop, and then Alice's crumbly building and the one next door, blinded where its windows should have been.

Rosie took the subway from Elmhurst, and over there all

the houses looked the same for blocks and blocks. Rosie's house wasn't that great, but she had a bedroom all to herself, with a blue-and-white-checked bedspread and matching curtains. Rosie said her mother made them. And she had a bathtub in the bathroom where it belonged, not in the damn kitchen.

Alice unlocked the door and Jamie followed her down the long hall. It smelled of stale smoke.

"We're home!" Alice called.

Claire was in her bathrobe, her elbows propped up on the kitchen table next to the overflowing ashtray. The sink was still filled with dishes from breakfast and from the night before. Everything was exactly as it had been in the morning when Alice left.

"Oh," Claire said. "Hi. You're back from school already? My gosh, is it three?"

"It's past five! I picked Jamie up."

"Oh. I guess the time just flew."

"It sure did," Alice said. "What the hell have you been doing all day?"

"Thinking . . ." Claire gestured vaguely. ". . . about things." She got heavily to her feet and opened the refrigerator door. "Let's see, there's some Velveeta left. You want some cheese?"

"You could've at least washed the dishes."

"I don't know. I've been so tired. And there's peanut butter and jelly. Make some sandwiches, Alice."

"I got a barbecued chicken."

"Oh. Well, that's good."

Alice took the chicken out of the bag. It was still pretty warm. She rummaged in the cabinet for clean plates.

"Hi, Mommy," Jamie said.

"Oh. Hi, hon. I'm so tired, Alice. I don't know. Maybe it's the flu or something. . . ."

"Yeah, sure." Alice sniffed at the milk in the container. It was still good. She poured two glasses.

"Mommy, you know what happened in school today?" Jamie said. "There was a big fight!"

Claire wandered back to her chair.

"And you know what? A kid got in trouble for fighting and . . . Mommy, a kid in the class. The teacher said—"

"Mmm-hmm," Claire said.

Alice was cutting up the chicken. "Go on, Jamie. What happened?"

"Nothin'." Jamie shrugged his shoulders. "That's all. Gimme the drumsticks."

"Take them."

Alice and Jamie took big hungry bites, gnawing right down to the bones. Claire picked at her piece with a knife and fork. Alice watched her. Claire was big on table manners, that and never cursing. She said "gosh" and "gee" and "oh, sugar" instead. That must be the way they talked in the Midwest. She'd done all those things—running away from home and hitching all the way east with Alice's father, only he went back west by himself before Alice was born—and she still hung on to putting her napkin in her lap and cutting little pieces with a knife and fork. Even chicken! And she was always saying you should have your good manners ready, like a habit, for when things turned around. But how in hell did she expect anything to change if she didn't even get washed in the mornings or get out of the house?

13

"You know what, Mommy?" Jamie said. "A lady told Alice to be a model."

"What?" Claire looked up.

Alice shot Jamie a look to keep quiet. She wanted to think about it some more by herself before getting Claire into it. But Jamie had Claire's attention and nothing was going to stop him now.

"She gave Alice a card and—"

"What? What kind of card?" Claire focused on him, suddenly alert.

"She gave Alice a card, that was when she called us back from the elevator, and she said . . . she said . . . about good bones and how old she was, that was before on the street, and . . ." Being in the spotlight made Jamie flustered, words tumbling out every which way. "The bag was heavy, but I carried it all the way and . . . uh . . . and . . . She said Alice ought to be a model!" he finished triumphantly.

"She didn't say 'ought to be.' She asked if I was interested, that's all."

"Why didn't you say something? Oh, wow, Alice! She gave you a card? Let me see."

"Alice, you promised an Almond Joy! Can I have an Almond Joy?"

"Okay. All right." Alice took the candy bars out of the grocery bag and put them on the table.

"This could be something, Alice! Let me see. . . ." Claire's eyes were bright and color was coming into her cheeks.

Jamie tore the wrapping and took a big bite, his eyes big and round, watching Claire. She was coming out of her low.

Mostly, it ran its course, but this time she was coming out of it real fast.

"Here." Alice dug the card out of her jeans pocket and handed it over. "It could be phony, Ma. It was so weird, the way it happened. . . ."

"Iris Martin Agency. That's no phony." Claire said the words slowly, thinking about them. "I've heard of it." She suddenly got up from the table. "Baby, this is it! This is our ship coming in! Didn't I tell you? Didn't I? I can feel my luck changing, right here, right now, right this very minute!"

Jamie caught Claire's mood. He started running around the table, brushing against their chairs, bumping into the stove. "Our ship's coming in! Our ship's coming in!"

"You got to do something." Claire was pacing up and down, crackling with energy. "You got to call right away. Quick."

"I can't, Ma. It's an office. It'd be closed now."

"Then first thing tomorrow."

"I'll be in school."

"Call from school! Honestly, Alice! You don't wait on a chance like this."

"It could be nothing. . . ."

Claire came around the table and took Alice's shoulders in her hands and talked straight at her. "You got to understand, sweetie. This is big! I was just reading the other day. That model, you know the one with the long blonde hair and the smile? She makes eight hundred thousand a year. A *year*. Come on, I'll show you." She went into the living room, Jamie running alongside, Alice trailing.

She rummaged through a pile of magazines and newspapers

in the corner. Jamie was helping, tossing newspapers on the unmade couch-bed.

"Here." Claire held up a copy of *Vogue*. "I'll show you. Wait. Here. This is the one."

Alice looked at the ad. The model was pretty, with big blue eyes. She slowly turned the pages, looking at the faces. Some of them were really beautiful. Boy, that was some hairdo, hair sticking out all over!

"I should have thought of this before. Gee, why didn't I ever think of it?" Claire's voice was a steady patter in the background.

"When's our ship coming in?" Jamie yelled. "When?"

Some of the faces weren't all that great. She had a nicer nose than that one, but . . .

Claire was leaning over her shoulder. "You look as good as any of them, baby. All you need is makeup."

. . . but they were all grown-ups, all sophisticated in furs and fancy dresses. They weren't kids. There was a kid on the Corn Flakes box, with freckles and her hair in cute little pigtails. Maybe that's the kind of thing the lady meant. Alice wondered if she could do that, looking healthy and vitamin-enriched. . . .

Jamie was racing around, jumping into the couch-bed and out again. "When? When? When?" He picked up a pillow and hurled it at Alice.

"I'll get you for that! I'll tickle you to death!" And she was running after him. He darted around the chair, sticking it in Alice's way, laughing. Alice threw the pillow at him and he threw it over at Claire. Claire caught it, laughing, with two bright pink spots on her cheeks. "The magazine! Don't step on the magazine!"

The room was too small and they kept running into things. Alice tackled him to the floor. She jumped on him and started tickling.

"No! Alice, stop! Come on, stop!" He was gasping, laughing, screaming.

And Claire got into it, rolling around with them. Their arms and legs were sticking out at angles, everybody tickling everybody. Then they were all sprawled out on the floor, out of breath, looking at each other and smiling.

"Oh, Ma," Alice sighed. Claire was irresistible when she was like this, all alive and sparkling. It was like when she was so sure her numbers were going to come up in Lotto. Claire's eyes would be shining, and Alice, knowing the odds were a million to one, couldn't help getting caught up, every time.

"You know who you're going to be, baby? You're going to be Alice in Wonderland. Only, when you go down the rabbit's hole, instead of getting smaller, you'll get bigger and bigger!"

Alice propped herself up on one elbow and looked at her curiously. "Was that your favorite book or something?"

"Your father liked it. He called it the ultimate acid trip. He used to read it aloud on the way east; he was so funny."

"Is that why you named me Alice?"

"I don't know. I don't remember now. It means 'smart' or 'joyful' or something like that. Anyway, it's a nice name."

"What does 'Jamie' mean, Mommy?"

"James was *your* father's name, that's all."

She could have said something better to him, Alice thought.

And from then on, Claire's high mood started getting irritating. She was talking fast and breathlessly about all the wonderful things they'd do and she got Jamie all hyper. And later, Alice had a terrible time getting him to bed. She had to keep promising that she'd go to bed soon, too, because he didn't like being in the room by himself. Claire was no help at all, watching and laughing, and Jamie kept bouncing out of bed. Finally, she got Jamie settled and all she wanted was to take a hot bath.

Claire followed her into the kitchen.

"You could clean the tub out once in a while." Alice was rubbing the ring with Ajax.

"You know what? I'll paint the kitchen tomorrow. How about red? Or yellow?"

"You better scrub the grease down first," Alice said. "No paint's gonna stick to that." She started running the hot water.

"Yellow's a happy color. What do you think, Alice?"

"I don't care."

"Something bright to celebrate. Bright yellow, like a taxi. . . ."

The tub was full. "Ma, I want to take my bath now."

"Go ahead. Listen, when you call tomorrow—"

"Ma, I want some privacy, okay?"

"I'm your *mother*. I used to *give* you baths. You getting shy all of sudden?"

Alice waited, her jaw set, while Claire poured herself some coffee. Finally, she took her cup and left, her voice trailing behind her. "Well, hurry out and we'll plan some more. Oh, everything's going to be so fine, sweetie. . . ."

18

Alice stripped down and put a toe in the water. It felt too hot, but if she edged in and got used to it, then it would be just right. She put her feet in and took the rubber band out of her hair and refastened it to hold her hair double, up on her head. Gingerly, she lowered her body, bit by bit. The steam felt good on her face and she slid all the way down. Her legs didn't fit. Her feet had to go over the edge. Someday, when she was rich, she'd have a big, long bathtub. When she was rich . . . Claire had said that model made eight hundred thousand a year. Eight hundred thousand. How many pairs of jeans go into eight hundred thousand? How many bikes? How much could she spend every day before she used it all up?

She was letting herself get sucked into some dumb pipe dream again.

She looked at her body under the water. Her breasts were too small; that's why she didn't want Claire to see. There was nothing good about her body. Her legs were too thin and they went on and on. She looked like a damn stork. If she called and they took a good look at her, they'd laugh and send her away. No one ever dropped dead on the street when she came walking by. She was no million-dollar model.

The water was perfect now and she leaned her head back and closed her eyes. Her skin was all warm and rosy. She'd start washing later. No rush. Nothing to worry about. Maybe she'd call and maybe she wouldn't.

3

Alice walked to school with Claire's last words still echoing in her ears. "Call right away, hon, first thing, before they forget all about you." Well, it didn't have to be the *very* first thing. Maybe after lunch. Maybe she'd tell Rosie about it and see what she thought.

She walked past the Roosevelt Island Tram and then west toward Third Avenue, caught in the swirl of going-to-work pedestrians. She looked sideways at her reflection in the window of the coffee shop. She wasn't even the prettiest girl at school. That was Laurie. Laurie was petite, with curly blonde hair and a bouncy way about her.

Past Dry Dock. Once she had seen a model right around here, trying to get a cab in the rain and looking all rushed and upset. You could always tell a model. Alice tried to figure out what it was—maybe the way they were made up or maybe the big cases they carried. She wished there was one around now, so she could check out the look. It was a definite look all right, wherever it came from.

Past Benetton. All of Claire's big talk about modeling made her jittery. Alice didn't like things suddenly coming along to confuse her life plan. Her life plan was good and straightforward. At Design Trades, she was learning how to letter and do paste-ups and layout, and she'd get a sure job right after graduation. She was glad she went to vocational school; they even had job placement. She had no time for fooling around with art; back in junior high, the art teacher had said she was talented and she'd wanted her to apply to LaGuardia—but that was college prep! It was good to have a trade. Rosie thought so, too.

A car horn honked in front of her and a taxi made a quick right turn against the light. Boy, you had to watch out all the time!

She had told Rosie the other part of the life plan that time when she'd slept over. They were lying on Rosie's bed in the morning, looking out at the sky past the blue-and-white-checked curtains. Alice was going to get legally married to a steady guy with a regular job, something solid like Civil Service—none of those flashy fly-by-nights for Alice Lonner—and someday they'd even put a deposit down on a house like Rosie's, someplace in Queens maybe. She'd keep it neat as a pin.

"But what about love?" Rosie had said.

Rosie liked to talk about love all the time, ever since she'd started going out with Mike. He lived right down her block and they were always hanging out together.

What was love anyway? The way Frank McCall made her feel? He was about the cutest boy in school and he had taken Alice to the movies twice. He'd kissed her, more times in a row than she'd ever been kissed—they didn't get to see anything of the movies—and it was nice. But later, they didn't have anything much to talk about.

Between thinking so hard and looking in store-window reflections, Alice made it to school just after the first bell. No time for phone calls. Then, when she saw Rosie at lunch, everyone else was around, too, chattering about all kinds of stuff, and Frank McCall was horsing around, ignoring her. Alice was halfway through her tuna fish sandwich before she got a chance to talk to Rosie without anyone else listening.

"This really funny thing happened," Alice said. "Some lady asked if I want to be a model."

"Oh?"

"What do you think? You think I could be a model?"

"Sure. You got to be tall." Rosie was chewing her Devil Dog and some of the white filling showed on her lips. "You know my cousin Gloria? The one in Brooklyn? She's a model."

"She is?" Rosie had so many cousins, always getting married or having babies or first communion or something.

"It's pretty good, too. Did you ever hear of Levine Coats and Suits?"

"No."

"It's on 38th Street, you know, in the garment center? She models for them. Do you know how to type?"

"A little," Alice said. "Not very fast."

"Oh. Gloria has to type and relieve the switchboard, too. Mostly, she models, when the buyers come in. And she gets a whole lot off on any coat she wants. She's been there a year and she's got a whole lot of good stuff."

Claire had said that the Iris Martin Agency was for magazine cover girls. Alice felt funny about saying anything about that now. She finished her sandwich in silence. She didn't want to sound like she thought she was better than Gloria.

"Hey, Alice, Gloria's twenty and those are full-time jobs. Do you want me to ask her about it, anyway?"

"No. No thanks. I was just thinking. . . ." She really did want to talk to Rosie and hear what she thought about it. Maybe another time.

Maybe Claire was all wrong again. But it wouldn't hurt to find out, not expecting anything, just to see. Just to stop wondering. It didn't have to change her life plan.

"Do you have change of a dollar?" Alice said. "I've got to make a phone call."

Alice followed Claire through the door of the Iris Martin Agency, into the confusion of the crowded reception room. It was filled with girls, girls standing and girls on the couches. They looked older and sophisticated, some of them were beautiful, there were a lot of people talking. . . .

Even Claire hesitated for a minute and then she plowed ahead. "Come on, baby. Tell them you're here."

There was a desk and a plump, dark-haired girl behind it. Alice had to wait her turn.

"I'm here to see Iris Martin."

"You and who else?" the girl said, without looking up. "Everybody gets screened by Pat Richards first. Fill out a card."

"Pat Richards told me to come. She said I'm supposed to see Iris Martin at one."

"Pat Richards sent you? Name?"

"Alice Lonner."

The girl brushed some papers off her calendar. "You're right, Lonner at one." She looked up for the first time and shrugged apologetically. "It's a cattle-call day, I didn't realize—"

"Cattle call?"

Her tone became friendly and confidential. "Tuesday, open audition. Wayne's out of town, so Pat's seeing everyone and we're kind of jammed up. You know, total chaos. . . ." She pushed a button on her phone. "Iris's one o'clock is here. Lonner." She handed Alice a card. "I guess you should fill this out, anyway. Have a seat."

There was no space left on the couches. Alice stood on the side, near Claire. She was glad she wasn't all alone. She felt awkward in Claire's best blouse. It was too ruffly. She wasn't going to wear it and then she thought maybe Claire was right and now she was sorry. Her wrists looked bony, sticking out of the ruffles on the sleeves. And some of these girls were really beautiful.

She glanced at Claire. Claire was wearing her all-out best makeup. The bright strokes of blusher stood out against her pale skin.

Alice filled out the card, propping it against the wall. Name. Address. Age. Height. Weight.

A good-looking girl with silken blonde hair brushed past her to return her card to the receptionist.

"Sorry. You're too old."

"What? Just how old do you think I am? I'm twenty-one!"

"Iris Martin policy. We never start anyone past eighteen."

"That's incredible! Look, I've been modeling in St. Louis for a year, I have pictures, I was Miss Missouri in—"

"Try Elite or Ford."

"Let me speak to Pat Richards!"

"Forget it."

The girl angrily swept up her portfolio and slammed the door.

Miss Missouri! Alice had never even thought of being "Miss" anything and she didn't have a portfolio. What was she doing here? All she had was the yearbook picture from when she graduated junior high. She remembered the photographer saying, "Cheese and crackers." Pat Richards had said to bring a photograph.

As their names were called, one by one, girls went down the hall to Pat Richards's office. Most of them were out again in minutes. One of them was crying openly. There's no way I'll cry, Alice thought, the hell with it. But she *had* passed the first screening, even if it was out on the street, and the receptionist had talked to her as if she belonged more than any of the others. When she looked around more coolly, Alice thought the competition wasn't so fantastic—she could look as good as that redhead if she had clothes like that, or that brunette, if she knew how to put on false eyelashes, and that one, over there, was fat. . . . She looked at Claire, who had found a seat across the room, and wondered if she was thinking the same things. Alice caught her eye and smiled.

And then She came in. She was elegant, exquisite, moving across the room sleek and fast as a greyhound. She was wearing a plain trench coat and jeans, but she was the instant center of the room.

"Hi," she said to the receptionist, oblivious to all the stares. "I'll just run in and see Pat—"

"There's somebody with her, give her a minute. How was it?"

"Outrageous! Utter madness! Milan is even better than Paris. But Giorgio was absolutely insane— They rigged Monica up to *fly* over the runway, can you imagine, *Monica!*— And he changed everyone's makeup after they'd worked on us for hours. They rehearsed us until midnight and there was no place left to *eat*, and oh, that *dolce vita!*" Her laugh rang through the suddenly silent room. "I'll be sleeping for days."

Then she disappeared into the inner sanctum, and the buzz resumed. "The Italian showings," someone said, and "That was Bambi," in tones of awe.

Alice's little bubble of confidence evaporated. She'd been dreaming; the competition wasn't out here at all! It was Bambi, girls like Bambi! It wasn't fair. Bambi made her feel so unpolished. Mabye teenage models were different. Maybe. She clutched the card and the envelope with her photograph in damp hands. I don't give a damn, she told herself. At least, she hadn't yesterday, not really. But the tension and the pent-up desire in this room were contagious, and now Alice ached with wanting. And it wasn't even for all the money Claire kept talking about. She wanted to belong to this exclusive club, with Bambi and Milan and doors opening automatically.

"Alice Lonner?" someone said.

"Yes, yes, here we are." Claire jumped up quickly to Alice's side.

"I'm Miss Martin's secretary. She's still tied up, but you can wait upstairs. Follow me, please."

Every face in the room turned to Alice. She could feel their looks, their hostile "What's she got?" looks. Well, Pat Richards had picked her out! And she was wearing Claire's beautiful blue eye shadow! She forced her head up and walked right past them, trying hard not to look scared.

4

The upstairs waiting room was smaller and nicer. It was thickly carpeted and there were little curved chairs.

Claire and Alice were alone except for the secretary behind her desk. The repetitious clatter of the typewriter was a backdrop to Claire's chatter. She was alternating between pep talks and last-minute advice, her hand gripping the back of Alice's chair.

They'd been sitting there for a long time. Waiting so long took the edge off Alice's tension. She felt dull, her body sluggish with inactivity.

". . . and you're so beautiful, sweetie."

Alice hoped the secretary wasn't listening.

"Your father was a beautiful man. That's where you get it from. He was so . . ."

Yeah, sure. Alice had heard it all before.

". . . and you even have beautiful hands! See how long your fingers are, see how they taper at the ends—maybe they'll use your hands, like for Jergens lotion. You'll have to grow nails. Oh, gosh, that one's broken . . ."

A dull ache was starting at the back of Alice's neck. She wished she had come alone. What did she ever come here for, anyway? She had cut Silk Screen Printing to get here on time and she had too many absences already. And now it was past two, and if they had to wait any longer, they wouldn't get home in time for Jamie. He had the key around his neck, but sometimes it jammed if he didn't get it in the lock right. He was so dopey sometimes. It was like he didn't trust them to come back.

The typewriter clacked, stopped for a moment, then started again.

The ache was getting worse, like one of those headaches when a test took too long and the classroom was stuffy. If she had any sense, she'd tell that secretary they had some nerve, making her wait this long, and then she'd just go and walk out. But she sat rooted to her chair, too out-of-place to move without being told.

"Miss Martin will see you now," the secretary said.

Alice tried to walk in cool, who-cares-anyway, but the office was a blur of white and long airy window views. The desk was up on a pedestal, and Alice, intimidated, stopped in front of it, on the lower level.

Iris Martin was so very beautiful, with pale blonde hair, framed by the white flowers on her desk. When she greeted them, when she told Claire to have a seat, she was smiling, and every word was clear and clipped. And Alice, left standing with her arms dangling, despaired of ever speaking that well or being that polished.

"Pat Richards said you had strong possibilities. Let's see. Yes, lovely cheekbones, good wide-spaced eyes. Mmm-hmm, Pat might be right; a baby Magdalena in the rough. . . ."

A what? She was afraid to ask.

Iris Martin tapped a pencil on the desk and examined Alice, thinking, deciding. "How tall are you?"

"Five eight," Alice said. "Oh, here's the card." She'd forgotten about the card she'd filled out downstairs. She handed it over with a too-abrupt motion.

"That's what I thought. That's a little short." Her frown chipped away at Alice's last little bit of confidence.

"Short? She's very tall for her age. She always has been." Claire's voice behind Alice sounded breathless and she was laughing a little, for no reason at all. "I mean, five eight, for her age. She's really five eight and a half. She's always growing. She grows right out of her clothes as soon as we buy them and—"

Miss Martin cut her off. "Height five eight, weight one fifteen." She was reading from the card. "Mmmm. You could lose five pounds."

Miss Martin reached into her desk drawer and pulled out a tissue. She came around the desk and wiped Alice's eyelids with it. Alice started at being touched so suddenly.

"That's much better. Never wear such a bright color, dear. It completely dominates your eyes."

30

Up close, there were little lines in Miss Martin's face. She reached for Alice's hair and rubbed it between her fingers.

"The texture is good. We'd have to do something with it, of course. As for the color—"

"Anything you say," Claire said. "Any color is fine."

Miss Martin crossed back behind her desk and sank into her chair. She stared and Alice felt exposed.

"Take off your jeans, dear."

"What?"

"I have to see your legs. You should have worn a skirt, you know."

Alice stood motionless. She couldn't take her jeans off, not in front of everybody! She looked helplessly at Miss Martin. The pencil tapped impatiently.

"You could be knock-kneed, for all I know."

Alice remembered that her underpants were thin and gray from too many washings. Some of the elastic was torn. And she couldn't take her clothes off, just like that, in somebody's office! Alice turned and looked beseechingly at Claire sitting behind her. Why didn't she speak up *now* and say something, something like, "No, leave her alone."

"Don't waste my time, dear," Miss Martin said.

And then Claire came to life. "For heaven's sake, Alice! Hurry up!"

Alice turned away, her lips tight. Thanks a lot, Ma! She unzipped the jeans and the sound was too loud. She bent down awkwardly to step out of them. They wouldn't go over her shoes. She should have taken her shoes off first. Her fingers fumbled with the laces. They were watching her. Standing on one leg and then the other, she pulled the jeans off. The torn elastic was hanging down.

The pencil tapped. "Socks, too, dear."

Alice bent again and rolled down the tube socks, not looking at anything, making herself go blank. Finally, she was bare-legged, numb and feeling gooseflesh.

"What is that on your knee?"

It was that little triangular scar, from the time she'd climbed over that fence and some wire had caught her. . . .

"A scar," Alice mumbled.

Under Miss Martin's stare, it became a huge deformity. She frowned. "Too bad."

Alice thought of the women in the supermarket, squeezing one fruit or another, discarding the bruised ones, looking for perfection. So she was an imperfect one. Okay. She didn't need someone looking her over like that. It was damn rude, that's what! She wanted to get her jeans on and go home.

"I suppose it could be covered. Are there any other scars I should know about? Anywhere on your body?"

"No."

"You do have nice legs, dear. Let me see your teeth. Smile."

Alice opened her mouth and turned up her lips.

"Good. You can get dressed now."

Alice pulled the jeans on quickly and slid her feet into the security of her shoes.

"I do wish you were taller." The pencil tapped, tapped. "Did you bring a picture with you?"

"Here. Here it is." Claire rushed forward to put the photograph on the desk.

32

"This is worthless. We'd have to see what a real photographer can do with you. . . . You should photograph well. You have magnificent bone structure." Iris smiled and Alice felt hope leaping up, jumping for every crumb of approval.

"Let me see you walk across the room. Slowly. Smaller steps, please."

How was she supposed to walk with someone watching every single footstep! She remembered to hold her head high.

"That's fine," Miss Martin said. Alice had reached the far side of the room, near the wall of photographs. "The one on the right is Magdalena. Pat Richards was very struck by your resemblance. The camera certainly loved her. . . ."

Alice studied the blow-up of the starkly beautiful face. Magdalena had very high cheekbones like hers, lit to emphasize the hollows underneath, but otherwise she was someone from another world. She was a sophisticated *woman!*

"Of course, she had those incredible green eyes. Oh, those eyes and that great mass of dark hair! Let's see, yours are brown, aren't they?"

So my eyes are brown and I have a scar, Alice thought, so what? But she was greedy for another smile from Miss Martin, another sign.

Claire had come up behind Alice to look at the photograph.

"It's the high cheekbones, isn't it?" Claire said. "That's from Alice's father. He was part Indian, you know, with that bone structure they have."

Alice shot Claire a look. How could she keep coming up with things like that! He was Irish the last time Alice heard, and anyway, Miss Martin couldn't have cared less!

"Alice, do you want to be a model? Badly enough to work at it?"

"Yes," Alice said. Was she supposed to say something more? Not badly enough to start gushing, Alice thought, not badly enough to get down on my knees for it. Oh, but she wanted— she wanted *something!*

"Why don't you both sit down and we'll talk a little." Miss Martin put down the tapping pencil and folded her hands on the desk. "We see thousands of lovely girls every year, and only a handful have what it takes to become an Iris Martin girl. Alice, you may have potential; you might work out. . . ."

Iris Martin was choosing her, one of the chosen few!

"If we take you on, it would be on a probationary basis, of course. First, we'd have to get some test shots and . . . The agency would be investing a great deal of time and money in you. We'd expect total discipline and commitment in return."

"Yes," Alice breathed.

"Very well. Start on the diet immediately." Miss Martin handed her a white sheet. "You're to follow it to the letter. If it says broccoli, you eat broccoli. No substitutions. Understood?"

"Yes, Miss Martin."

"Call me Iris, dear. We're one big family here."

"Yes, Iris," Alice said and suddenly realized that the white flowers on the desk were irises. How fantastic!

Miss Martin—Iris—smiled at Claire. "I'm den mother to all my girls. We have girls from Europe, Scandinavia, one from Australia, and their families know they can entrust them to my care. Rest assured that Alice will be in the very best hands. She's underage, of course, so if you'll sign these forms, Mrs. Lonner. Our commission is twenty percent, which is standard, and Alice is to work exclusively for this agency. Fine, thank you. Now this one is for a work permit and . . ."

A wave of belonging swept over Alice. She was in the club and Iris would take care of her.

"All right, then. We can get started." Iris checked her calendar and pushed the intercom button. "Myra, set up an R&D for Alice Lonner, Thursday at two."

"An R&D?" Alice asked.

"Research and Development conference. We'll decide how to package you. There's a lot to do before your first go-see."

"Go-see?"

"You'll go-see photographers for test shots for your composite, and once you have that, your go-sees will be job interviews. I'll probably assign you to Billie—your booker will explain our procedure."

"Would my jobs be—like for *Seventeen* or—"

"No, no, you're definitely not a junior type. No, you're an exotic, dear. High fashion, more along the lines of a Magdalena."

Alice was stunned. It was all a mistake. Maybe Iris hadn't read everything on the card. "I'm only fourteen," Alice said hesitantly.

"Yes, youth is a great asset," Iris said. She smiled and rose to dismiss them. "I'll see you here on Thursday at two, Alice."

"Oh. But I'm supposed to be in school—"

"Make whatever arrangements are necessary. Perhaps a tutor. Or arrange your school schedule for mornings only.

35

That would give you a good block of time in the afternoon. This agency is your priority and I'm sure you can work it out." "No problem," Claire said. "No problem at all. She'll be here. Oh, thank you. Thank you so much!"

Claire bubbled all the way out—through the hall, down the stairs, past the crowd still waiting in the reception room. "We did it, baby!" She whirled Alice around on the street. "We did it!"

"Ma, she said I'm not a junior. Ma, I don't know *how* to be a grown-up."

"Oh, Alice! Wonderland, here we come!"

It was all coming true, the whole crazy pipe dream, with contracts and irises on a desk and— She should have been whirling around with Claire, spinning wildly in triumph and excitement. She was stopped by the sensation underneath: clammy, paralyzing, unreasoning, heart-thumping fear.

5

When the alarm woke her, Alice knew there was something hanging over her—and then it all came flooding in. She had to talk to the guidance counselor to see if she could get afternoons off. Maybe she'd even have to argue with the principal and he'd say school came first. . . . And then there was that R&D thing on Thursday. Research and Development. What was she supposed to do there? Her stomach hurt.

"Jamie," she yelled. "Come on, get up! I mean *now* if I'm gonna walk you! I can't be late again."

Finally, he was up and getting washed. She heard the couch in the living room squeaking. Claire must be awake—a sure sign that her low was really over.

Alice rifled through the dresser drawer. "Hey, Ma! How about splurging on some underwear? All my pants are torn! All the elastic's ripped!"

She heard Jamie splashing at the sink.

"Ma! How'm I supposed to go to that R&D with torn pants?"

"Okay, sweetie," came muffled from the living room. "I'll see if I can get some."

"You better," Alice muttered. What if they wanted her to take off her jeans again?

Then later, as she was pulling Jamie out the front door, no time to even look in the refrigerator, Claire handed her a dollar.

"Here," she said. "Get yourselves some jelly doughnuts on the corner."

Alice whirled around, furious. "What are you talking to me about jelly doughnuts for? I'm supposed to be on the diet! I'm supposed to have a damned boiled egg!" Why couldn't Claire do anything helpful like some normal mother!

She knew she was screaming, but all Claire said was, "Oh. Sorry."

The irritation lasted all the time she walked Jamie to his school. Then she felt bad all the way to Design Trades because she'd yelled at him. And she still had to go talk to the guidance counselor. . . .

Mrs. Fishman didn't know her from Adam. There were so many kids assigned to her, and unless she set the school on fire, how would Mrs. Fishman remember her, anyway, just from that one appointment at the beginning of the term? Mrs. Fishman had been shuffling papers and folders, never looking up, never listening to Alice at all, going on and on about too many absences. . . .

This time, though, Mrs. Fishman was smiling at her, her

fat cheeks quivering a little. She was looking right at Alice, eye to eye, really seeing her face.

"I don't see why not, dear," she said, smiling all the way. She had shown instant recognition at the mention of the Iris Martin Agency. "It's lucky you have a late lunch. If we switch you to the morning section for English and . . . let's see, you could possibly drop Graphic Art I. . . ."

Drop Graphic Art? She liked it! She was *good* at it! "But—would I get an F?"

"No, no, you could take an Incomplete and make it up next term. . . ."

How would she ever make it up? Design Trades was important to her *life plan*, maybe the modeling wouldn't work out at all, maybe she wouldn't even like it, and now she'd miss the rest of Graphic Art. . . .

"That would free up your afternoons, except for Friday. . . . Could you work around that, four afternoons instead of five?"

"I think so," Alice said. Whoa, Alice thought, this was too easy.

Mrs. Fishman was writing on the schedule. "I'm glad we could accommodate you—thank heaven for that late lunch!"

Now that she had all those afternoons free, what if she didn't get any jobs at all? Iris Martin had said "probationary basis." Alice took a deep ragged breath.

"I don't think I can get the changes through until next week. Is that all right?"

"Yes," Alice said, "except for this Thursday. I have to be there Thursday afternoon."

"I'll give you an excused absence, if you'll make up the work. How's that?"

"That's fine," Alice said. "Thank you, Mrs. Fishman."

Mrs. Fishman was beaming. "It's just wonderful, dear. Design Trades will be so proud of you. Be sure to stop in and let us know how you're doing."

"Iris Martin Agency" were the magic words, all right. It was so different from when they'd given her all that grief the time Jamie was throwing up and she took some days off. How come taking care of a sick kid was no excuse and this R&D thing made it okay?

6

The secretary said, "Go on in. They're all there."

It sounded like a crowd. Alice wondered if there would be a whole lot of grown-ups asking her questions. And what was Research and Development, anyway?

Alice turned the doorknob slowly. *Who cares, so what, I don't give a damn,* she told herself and she lifted her chin as she opened the door.

Iris Martin was wearing something soft and fuzzy in deep lilac. She was just as beautiful as Alice had remembered.

"Here she is. This is Alice Lonner," Iris said. "Alice, you know Pat Richards, of course."

It was good to see a familiar face. Pat smiled encouragingly.

"And this is Billie Liebman. Billie will be your booker." Billie didn't look elegant like the others. She was plump and in rolled-up shirt sleeves. "And my assistant, Wayne Hannigan." Iris talked fast, clipping the words. "Would you like some coffee, dear?"

"No, thanks."

"All right, then, sit down and let's get started."

Alice sat in the same chair as the last time. It was below the raised area of the desk. The others were close around the huge white desk, coffee cups in front of them. Maybe she should have asked for coffee. Maybe then she'd be in the middle of everyone, not set apart like this, facing them.

"Well," Iris said, "What do you see?"

"I see a blank slate," Wayne said. "A schoolgirl with too much hair."

"Really? That's all?"

"Okay, she looks a little like Magdalena—but that does not a Magdalena make," Wayne said.

Then Pat Richards was talking. "When I found her she had her hair pulled back. Alice, hold your hair back. More, back from your face. That's better. . . . Now! Is this a baby Magdalena or isn't it?"

"I don't know," Wayne said.

Alice wondered if she was supposed to keep holding her hair. Wayne was still looking at her. That day at the Food Emporium, she'd pulled it back with a rubber band, any which way. Today, she'd gone to a lot of trouble to comb it out just right. She'd even curled the front. And now she was stuck with her hands at her head, wrecking it.

"She has potential," Wayne said, "but forget the Magdalena look. Maggie left—what? ten years ago?—and no one's going to care." He chuckled. "Except John Alveira."

That drew an answering laugh from everybody. What was so funny about John Alveira? And Wayne was staring at her. If anyone stared at her that way in the subway or at school, she'd make some kind of wise-ass remark. "Yell when you see something green." She never put up with anything from anybody! But these people treated her like she was dumb and meek, and she couldn't help being exactly the way they had typed her.

"Actually," Iris said, "I thought I'd send her to John for test shots."

"It would be interesting to see what he gets from her," Pat said. "*If* he'll do it."

"I'll speak to him," Iris said. "He'll do it."

They were all talking and no one said anything to her.

"Let's get back to the hair," Iris said. "Long or short?"

It seemed rude for them to be talking about her as if she wasn't even there. She'd think it was damn rude—but then, they were the kind of people who'd know how to act. . . .

"She needs some distinction," Wayne said. "Nothing bland. I could see a short, shiny, straight cap, bangs maybe, almost circa Louise Brooks."

"I know what you mean," Pat put in. "But I think long would be—"

"I agree with Wayne," Iris said. "Short and geometric. But no bangs. And very contemporary. . . ."

"Mmmm. Yes," Wayne said.

"And a lot of contrast," Iris continued. "Blacken the hair, dye the eyebrows and eyelashes. . . ."

"She has fair skin," Pat said. "Whiten it and—"

"God, anything to get rid of that schoolgirl look!" Wayne lit a cigarette with a heavy silver lighter.

"Does that sound like Damian to everyone?"

"Definitely," Wayne said. "He'll do that *bruised* look around the eyes."

"His look *sauvage*," Pat put in.

"Damian it is, then." Iris turned to Alice. "We'll send you to Damian for makeup and hair."

"I'd like to keep my hair long," Alice said hesitantly. It had taken forever to grow and Frank McCall said he liked long hair and . . .

Iris's mouth curved into a smile that didn't reach her eyes. "Trust our judgment, dear. And you can always add pieces for versatility."

"Let me see your teeth, please," Wayne said.

Alice drew up her lips. They were shaking a little.

"Send her to Dental Art," Wayne said. "If the canines are shaved a bit and the front teeth lengthened—"

"Do you know what Jeff is asking these days? Six hundred dollars per tooth!" Iris frowned. "I'm not prepared to go for bonding now. Let's see how she does first."

Was there something wrong with her teeth? God, she didn't want to go to a dentist!

"It made such a big difference for Ginny. She can finally smile," Wayne said.

"No, her teeth will do. Maybe later, if she works out."

"Did you see the spread Jeff had in *Vogue*? He's an absolute genius," Pat said.

"An expensive genius," Iris answered. "All right. What else? Alice, stand up."

44

"She could be taller," Wayne said.

"Yes," Iris agreed.

"Pat manages to find us the short ones," he said.

"Five eight." Pat looked angry. "That's not too bad. And she has such *strong* potential. She'd be a good de la Renta type. . . ."

"Yes," Iris said. "Billie, make a note to contact Oscar."

"Maybe she'll grow if you water her," Wayne said. "Well, at least she's thin, not like the Berlin Bombshell."

They all laughed, all except Billie who gave Alice a sympathetic look.

"Are you following the diet I gave you, Alice?" Iris said. "I did think five pounds off."

They didn't even give her a chance to answer!

"Maybe a little more," Wayne said. "Emphasize those wonderful bones."

Pat looked happier. "It was the cheekbones that I spotted. And the walk."

"Marvelously arrogant," Wayne said.

Iris smiled at Alice again. "Go downstairs with Billie, dear. She'll explain the routine to you."

Billie got up. Was it over that fast? Alice knew that they'd be talking about her after she left. She concentrated on holding her head up and walking—arrogantly?—as she followed Billie out of the office.

The downstairs room was messy and cluttered, in complete contrast with the luxury of Iris's immaculate office. There were rows of desks, phones ringing, many voices talking at once. Billie's desk was at the end, overwhelmed by the huge bulletin board over it. There were large charts tacked to the board, with names and time slots and a lot of scribbles.

"Relax," Billie said. She indicated the chair for Alice and, pushing a pile of papers over, sat on a corner of the desk.

Alice sank down into the chair and let out a deep breath she hadn't even known she was holding.

Billie grinned. "Gruesome, wasn't it?" She seemed friendly, like a regular person. There were deep dimples in her full cheeks. "Come on, it wasn't *that* bad."

"He said I was a blank slate."

"Don't worry about Wayne. He's always doubtful about Pat's discoveries—but his suggestions are worth gold. He has a good eye for what sells. And Damian will do a great job on you. You'll like it, you'll see."

Alice shrugged.

"Hey, you're a very lucky girl! This agency is the best, for God's sake! . . . So, let's get to work. I'll set up your appointment with Damian. How's tomorrow?"

"You see, I have to be in school tomorrow until three. I have all the other afternoons free. Just not Fridays. . . ."

"Right, school. How old are you?"

"Fourteen. Nearly fourteen and a half."

Billie groaned. "God! Another year and a half before you can quit!" She sighed. "All right. I'll block out Fridays until three. For now, anyway." She was making notes on a pad.

"I'm sorry, I—"

"Can't be helped—stupid state law. I'll try to get Damian for Monday. The sooner the better. Call me to confirm. I'm your contact here, okay? You call my line every afternoon to see what I've got for you. That's important because I don't

46

have time to be tracking you down. All right. Stop in after Damian gets through and I'll get your weight and statistics then. Who knows, maybe you can lose some over the weekend. And I'll have your go-see list."

The telephone rang. "Billie Liebman. Oh, Jessica, hi. How's it going?" She squinted up at one of the charts. "You've got Polaris at two and Magnuson at four-thirty. . . . What?. . . Well, try to make it as soon as you can, doll. And listen, Young and Rubicam is seeing girls for that shampoo thing on Monday at ten. Fourth floor. That's right, Monday. . . . All right, talk to you later. Good luck, Jess." She hung up. "Sorry. Where were we?"

"My go-see list."

"Right. Photographers for you to see in the hope they'll do test shots. Now that's important, so make nice. We have to get a portfolio together before I can send you out on anything. You go right down the list and try to cover as many as you can, as fast as you can."

"Okay."

"Then, when you do get work, be sure to get a voucher after every job and turn it in to me. That way, you get paid at the end of the week and you don't have to wait for the billings to come through."

"A voucher?" Alice said.

"Don't worry. It'll all make sense as you go along. You live in town, don't you? You live with your family?"

"Yes," Alice said.

"Well, at least you're not out of some hick town and in the city all by yourself. Now that's confusion! You'll be fine. So, what else do you want to know?"

"How much. . . I mean, what can I expect?"

"In terms of money? Anybody's guess. Of course, you have to go over a certain amount for Iris to keep you on. You might not have any work at all for weeks, at least at the beginning. On the other hand, if you do very well, you could make more than a brain surgeon. . . . Look, I really have to get back on the phones. Any last questions?"

"Well, yes. . . . They kept talking about Magdalena."

"No, you wouldn't know, would you? She must have been at her peak before you were born. They called her the 'face of the Sixties,' but she was unique; she didn't belong to any particular time. We're talking *legend* here. She lasted right through her thirties. She was still here when I started working for Iris."

"Is she dead now or what?"

"Hell, no, not Maggie! She married some count and took off."

"And who's John Alveira?"

"A dynamite photographer. His shots of Maggie were spectacular. He was just a kid from someplace, New Bedford or someplace, when Maggie found him. They lived together for a while, one of those autumn-May things. She did a lot for him, introduced him around, got his career started, but she sure took a chunk out of him when she left."

"He's a kid?"

Billie laughed. "Not any more. This all goes back more than ten years. He won't be on your list; Iris will talk to him personally and try to set something up." Billie looked at Alice speculatively. "He just might be interested. . . ."

7

After school on Friday, Alice and Rosie stopped in front of the building, hesitant to separate, forcing the stream of kids rushing out to detour around them. They'd been having a good conversation, mostly about Frank McCall and Laurie.

"Laurie's not *that* great," Rosie said.

Alice knew Rosie was being loyal. Everyone thought Laurie was the prettiest girl in the school. She didn't have *bones*, though. She had a soft, roundish face with beautiful eyes, but her cheekbones didn't show.

It bothered Alice to see Frank kidding around with Laurie all the time, especially after those two times at the movies. Maybe if she'd had more to say to him. . .

"All the boys like her," Alice said.

Laurie was no more than five two. Iris Martin would never

sign her on. The girl everyone thought was the prettiest couldn't ever be a model, but she, Alice Lonner, could! And that's when Alice told Rosie all about the Iris Martin Agency and everything that had happened. Everything except the part where they were talking about her as if she wasn't there.

Rosie's eyes were big and round. "That's not like my cousin Gloria! You're talking about ads and stuff!"

"I guess," Alice said. She felt Rosie studying her face, her features.

"Wow! You know something? We've got to talk some more." Rosie shifted her books to her other arm. "How come you didn't say anything?"

"I didn't know if it was set for sure and—"

"You must be so psyched!"

Alice had been a sleepwalker in a daydream, but telling Rosie made it real. Rosie's reaction excited her.

"I can't wait to see how that Damian does you!"

"He's supposed to cut my hair short. I never wanted it short before, but—"

"They let Christie Brinkley and Cheryl Tiegs have long hair, so . . ."

"I'm supposed to be an *exotic* and . . ."

"And you'll be wearing all those clothes and . . ."

They talked and talked, interrupting each other, words tumbling on top of each other. Rosie was so solidly in her own life, with Mike and her family and everything, that she could be honestly enthusiastic, with no sour edges.

The kids rushing out had dwindled to a trickle. The sun was shining. It was an early-March false spring and Alice

50

imagined that she smelled fresh soil and growing things under the cement. Well, maybe it was from the scraggly tree in its iron cage on the sidewalk, timidly pushing out new leaves.

". . . and that lady discovering you like that, right on the street! . . ."

The last few stragglers were making their way up the avenue.

"I ought to be getting home," Alice said slowly, wanting to prolong the moment.

"No, wait. Come sleep over at my house. We'll talk some more. . . ."

The subway to Queens was crowded and they couldn't get seats. Alice held on to the overhead strap with one hand and clutched her overstuffed looseleaf binder with the other. Rosie leaned against a pole, her feet apart to keep her balance. With Alice in sneakers and Rosie in two-inch heels, they were almost the same height.

The train lurched and Rosie staggered a little, laughing. "Pretty soon we'll be *driving* to Elmhurst in your great big Caddy."

"Yeah, no more subways for us."

They were laughing and talking too loud. A middle-aged woman, her face drawn with fatigue, looked up from her newspaper with annoyance.

"Lady," Rosie said. "This is a cover girl!"

The woman shook her head in disgust. Rosie made a face at her, barely discernible, but Alice could tell and started giggling.

"Right," Rosie went on. "You'll roll up to my door in the limo, dragging your diamonds, and—"

"And emeralds." Alice was laughing, feeling a little delirious. "Big ones, on my ears and around my neck. No ring, though. That would make me look engaged, wouldn't it?"

"You know something? Seriously. You're gonna be meeting a lot of interesting guys, older guys. . . ."

"I don't know," Alice said.

"Oh, sure. You'll be in a whole different crowd."

The train had hurtled through the tunnel and was speeding on the overhead tracks. In the light coming through the windows, in the rays of dust, Rosie's face looked wistful.

"Get me into some of those parties, okay?"

"I don't know about any parties," Alice said. "I don't know if it's going to be like that."

"Sure it will. There are always models at those parties, you know, in Suzy's column, with rock stars and that whole crowd."

"Okay. If I get invited to something, I'll get you in."

"Alice? Do you think I could be a model, too?"

Alice loved Rosie's looks—a vivid complexion, lively dark eyes, a great smile—but she could see her through Iris's eyes. Nose pert, but a little wide. Hippy, with stubby legs.

"I'd have to lose—like ten, fifteen pounds?" Rosie looked embarrassed.

Alice felt uneasy. "I don't know that much about it yet."

The train rattled on and they were silent.

Rosie recovered the mood first. "Anyway, here's to emeralds and interesting guys and no more high-school jerks like Frank McCall!"

"Right on," Alice said, laughing too loud.

Rosie's block was a row of attached two-family houses, all identical red brick with tiny front areas just big enough to squeeze in a little tree or bush. They were the kind of houses that would fill Alice with yearning if she were passing by, wondering about the different kinds of lives going on inside.

Even before they went through the door, Alice could smell garlic and butter and anise. Rosie's mother really liked cooking. She had a whole closetful of cookbooks—Greek, Chinese, Italian, everything. It was like a hobby with her.

They went in and dropped their books on a chair.

"Hi! I'm home! Alice is sleeping over."

Mrs. Panagis poked her head through the kitchen doorway. "Hello, Alice, nice to see you. How's it going?" She disappeared again and there was the sound of running water. "Rosalie, turn on the front lights."

"Okay, but it's not dark yet."

"I have to call home," Alice said.

"Sure, go ahead."

Jamie answered the phone, a wavery "hello."

"Hi, Jamie."

"Alice, where are you? Where *are* you?"

"I'm at Rosie's. You know, my friend Rosie?"

"But when are you coming home?"

"I'm sleeping over here. Let me talk to Ma."

"She's not home. She's working. I'm all by myself."

"She didn't say anything this morning."

"She left a note." His voice was quivering. "It says 'I'm at work. Make peanut butter sandwiches.' "

53

"I didn't know, I'm sorry. . . . Jamie? She'll be home in a little while. It's almost five."

The sound of Jamie breathing at the other end.

"Jamie?"

"I'm all by myself and . . ." His voice was very small and faded out.

"Oh, Jamie. I'm sorry. I'm all the way over here already. . . . Look, tell Ma I'm sleeping over, and Jamie, I'll call you again in a little while, okay?"

"Alice?"

"Ma will be home soon."

"Okay, Alice." He was trying so hard to be brave! Alice could imagine him with his lips set tight so he wouldn't cry.

"We'll do something good when I get home. One afternoon soon, the two of us."

Silence.

"Did everything go all right in school today?"

"I lost my reader and then I found it."

"I want you to write down the number here."

"I don't got a pencil."

"Well, go get one."

A pause.

"I got a crayon."

"All right. Write it down. 718-555-5282. Got it?"

"Uh-huh."

"So's you can call me if you need to. And I'll call you in a little while and check on you. Okay?"

"Okay."

"All right then. See you later." Alice hesitated before she

hung up. She knew he was standing there, holding the phone. He wouldn't hang up until after she did. The sound of his voice made her feel worse than if he'd been crying.

"You are so lucky!" Rosie was back from turning on the outside lights.

"Me? Lucky?"

"All you have to do is say you're sleeping over and that's it. You know what my father does? He has to know the people where I'm staying and then he has to talk to the *parents*. He makes such a big production out of everything, it's embarrassing!"

"I guess everyone's different."

"You know what it is? He thinks I'd sneak off with Mike someplace." Rosie laughed. "Not that I wouldn't."

Rosie's older brother Nick came in, all dirty because he worked at a printer's, and he went to take a shower before dinner. Rosie's kid sister Diana drifted in and then the living room was full of the sound of television. Diana was flushed from playing outside with the kids on the block, and Alice thought how unfair it was for Jamie. It was a beautiful day and Jamie was cooped up all by himself with nothing to do. At that age, was a mother supposed to call another mother to arrange having a friend come over? Or was he old enough to do that himself? Jamie didn't have that many friends.

They had to wait for dinner until Mr. Panagis came home from work. When he did, everything revolved around him. Everyone came right away when he said to sit down at the table.

Dinner was a casserole of eggplant and ground meat, topped

with bubbling cheese; that's where the smell of garlic and anise had come from. And there were fried mushrooms and rice and a big salad studded with salty black olives. Alice remembered the Iris Martin diet. She was supposed to have half a grapefruit and a lean hamburger. Well, the ground meat in the casserole was something like a hamburger, wasn't it? Dinner at the Panagises' was too good to resist, and she could starve over the weekend to make up for it. She didn't take too much rice, though, and Mrs. Panagis noticed right away.

"Alice, you're not eating anything. Come on, have some more."

"Greek men love plump girls!" Rosie sang out.

"Don't get fresh, Rosalie," Mr. Panagis said sternly, passing the bread.

Everyone was talking at once. Nick had a problem with his boss, and Diana was all excited about getting the good-fairy part in her school play, and Mrs. Panagis was worried about her sister being sick, so Mr. Panagis said he'd call the doctor and find out exactly what's what. The talk flowed around Alice, and she felt warm and mellow.

Dessert was baklava, oozing with honey, and, except for Diana, they all had strong black espresso with a twist of lemon.

Mr. Panagis leaned back contentedly and said to Alice, "So, what's the good word, gorgeous?"

Alice never knew how to answer questions like that, so she smiled and shrugged.

"Alice has *big* news," Rosie said and told them about the modeling. Mrs. Panagis oohed and aahed, and Diana said,

"Wow! Like my Barbie Model Kit!" Even Nick looked interested.

"Now, listen, Alice." Mr. Panagis was frowning. "Go very slow on this. Have someone check it out before you sign anything. How much do you know about them?"

"Oh, Daddy!" Rosie said. "It's a famous agency!"

"I don't know," Mr. Panagis said. "I don't like the idea of taking a young kid—how old are you, Alice, fourteen, fifteen?—and painting her up and having her run around to photographers. I wouldn't want Rosalie to—"

"Oh, Daddy!"

"Make sure someone's looking out for your interests. You can't be too careful. Make sure no one's taking advantage."

Rosie made an exasperated face, but Alice liked the way he was acting concerned.

"Now, Gus," Mrs. Panagis said, "I'm sure Alice's mother has looked into it. She has, hasn't she?"

"Yes," Alice said. "Sort of."

"Well, I think it's just wonderful," Mrs. Panagis said. "Now you keep us posted on what's happening."

It was almost ten before Alice had a chance to call Jamie again. She waited until the Panagises had scattered; Alice didn't want anyone listening in case Claire hadn't come home yet.

Mike had come over and Rosie was concentrating on him in the living room. Mr. Panagis and Nick were glued to the TV. Mrs. Panagis was putting Diana to bed.

Alice was relieved to hear Claire answer the phone.

"Hi, Ma."

"Where in the world have you been, Alice? I found your

brother asleep on the floor in front of the door, waiting for you! And he made a mess with the peanut butter and—"

"Waiting for *me*? He was waiting for *you!*" Alice kept her voice in a tight whisper. "When did you get in?"

"I just now—"

"Oh, great! That's great!"

"Office Temps called me and then I stopped off for a while and . . . I expected you to be home and . . ."

Damn, oh damn! Jamie falling asleep on the floor like some little animal!

"I expected you to feel some obligation to—"

"Don't tell me obligation! He's not my kid, he's *your* kid, remember?" Alice's voice was a low hiss. She could tell by the silence at the other end that she had cut Claire the way she had meant to. "How was I supposed to know you'd be working? You barely make it out of bed!"

"That was before. I've been so . . . so much better." Claire's voice was shaking with the injustice of it. "I've been . . . feeling better for . . . for days now and . . ."

That was another thing. When Alice attacked, Claire and Jamie never stood up to her. They just folded when she let her anger out. So she was always stuck with either the anger or the guilt!

"Monday, I have to go for my hair and makeup—I don't know how long that'll take—and after that, I'm supposed to see photographers in the afternoons. I'm talking about every single day. I'll be busy. I'll be *busy* all the time. So you'd better shape up!"

"Don't put on airs with me, Alice. You haven't earned a penny yet."

"I'm not supposed to! I'm not even *supposed* to be working! I'm supposed to go to school, that's all! That's all I should be doing!"

Another long silence at the other end. Then, softly, "I do my best."

"I know, Ma," Alice said wearily. "I'll see you tomorrow."

She was glad none of the Panagises were around just then. Mrs. Panagis was probably reading a bedtime story or something to Diana. Oh, Jamie, she thought, you *are* my kid, you're my own little brother, I'll make it up to you, I will.

When the family went to bed, Alice, Rosie, and Mike hung out on the front stoop. Alice liked Mike. He wasn't really good-looking—he had red hair that stood up funny, and Rosie kept kidding him about it and pushing it back—but he had a nice, sort of quizzical look and he was fun. Alice could tell that he and Rosie were friends, along with all the other stuff. They were just hanging out, talking and listening to Mike's box, turned down low, when Mr. Panagis called through the window.

"Rosalie, come in now. It's past midnight."

"But there's no school tomorrow. . . ."

"I said come in. Now!"

Rosie and Mike kissed good night and stalled a little.

Mr. Panagis's voice came booming through the window. "Hey, Mike, don't you have a home to go to?"

"Okay, Mr. Panagis. I'm going. See you tomorrow, Rosie."

They watched him walk down the quiet street.

"See how my father is? It's too much!" Rosie exploded. "He's so bossy! Boy, women's lib sure hasn't made it to Elmhurst!"

"It's not women's lib he's worried about."

"Yeah, I know." Rosie sighed. "Maybe if Mike was Greek . . ."

The street was dark and peaceful. There was the faint sound of a dog barking far away. A breeze rustled the forsythia bush in front of the house. Mike turned and waved at them from a distance.

All of it—Mike down the block, the family sleeping, the faint cooking smells inside the front door, Mr. Panagis's strong presence in the house—made Alice feel so . . . *safe.*

8

On the way to her appointment with Damian at the Quintessence Salon, Alice pretended Mr. Panagis was her father. Rosie's dad would never let anyone push his kid around. That was an old trick she had—putting on someone else's skin when she needed to. And just in case this turned out to be like that R&D afternoon . . .

The first things that registered when she entered the long mirrored room were the bustle of the place and the loud, throbbing beat. It was ZZ Top with that song about every girl's crazy for a sharp-dressed man, loud good-time rock and roll. And then Damian was introducing himself, talking a mile a minute, and he was young, in his twenties, maybe. He was acting very friendly, nothing like that Wayne, and right away Alice let go of being Mr. Panagis's daughter.

Damian led her past a woman in a bright yellow parachute suit. Her hair was being combed out and she was frowning at a portfolio of photographs, biting her thumbnail.

"You think this is really the best one? Your absolutely honest opinion?"

"Definitely. Trust me, darling."

"But Tony, maybe the other one is . . ."

Alice followed Damian to an alcove. He was bouncing along in time to the music.

"Sit down, I can't wait to get started. This will be *fun!* I love working on Iris's exotics!" He talked in exclamation points.

He was thin, as thin as she was—she thought his skin-tight maroon pants would probably fit her. His shirt, collarless and silky, was a clashing shade of red that somehow looked right.

"Pretty girl, you are going to be a drop-dead stunner."

Alice smiled at him in the mirror. "What are you going to do?"

He snapped his fingers. "Magic." He ran his fingers through her hair and rubbed it between his fingertips. "Good hair. Iris wants black . . . mmmm, excellent. Black is the hardest color to get right. You know that phony blue-black look? All one dead color? I don't do that. I'll blacken selective strands, in three shades, and leave some natural dark brown. You'll have that jet-black effect, but it'll be alive."

"I don't know if I want it short, though," Alice said.

"I know how you feel. You've spent a long time growing it, right? But we do what Iris says. You need a distinctive, sophisticated . . . I see it short, pushed straight back at the sides, a little length at the nape and almost a cockscomb in the front, standing up, very electric . . . . Clear it off, let your face show, expose stark bones. It'll be fantastic!"

"Okay," Alice said. Suddenly, she couldn't wait to see how it would be.

"Aging you—that's pure pleasure. It is *bor*-ing to cover lines and . . . no, you're exactly the kind of job I love."

The tape changed to a piercing guitar solo.

"Get shampooed and then we'll get to work." Another man materialized at Damian's side. He had an entirely different face, but he was out of the same mold—young, thin, in skin-tight pants. "Brett, wash her and get numbers four, seven, and eight ready. Oh, that'll be stunning against your skin. Look at this skin—Devonshire cream!"

"Mmmm," Brett said. "She's divine."

"And the lips. Sculptured like Michelangelo's David."

Alice's hair was soaped. Her head was tilted way back and she felt Brett's fingers massaging her scalp. She closed her eyes and inhaled the sweet fragrance of the shampoo.

An urgent voice blared from the speakers.

> *Party time, let's party*
> *'Cause party time is runnin' out . . .*

Then she was back at Damian's station. His enthusiasm was contagious. He clipped and talked and did little dance steps. Her hair was wet and she couldn't tell what it would look like. She felt light-headed as more and more was clipped off.

> *If you don't want to party*
> *Don't come 'round tonight . . .*

63

"Don't look yet. Don't even think about it until it's dry and colored. And I'm going to dye your eyebrows and lashes. You ever hear that saying, 'God put her eyes in with a sooty finger'? That's how you'll look, thick black lashes top and bottom."

"I wish my eyes weren't plain brown," Alice said. "Magdalena had green eyes."

"Your eyes are *very* light brown, almost amber. Against the black, they'll look even lighter, and I'll do gold highlights. I'll give you tiger eyes. Gorgeous!"

"Was Magdalena's hair dyed too?"

"Magdalena? Wow. A bit before my time, you know?"

"Oh. Everyone keeps telling me about her. I'm supposed to look like her."

"She's past-tense. This is Alice Lonner time! You'll do great."

"I hope so."

He had finished cutting and he pulled a perforated bathing cap over her head. He pulled strands of hair through the holes with a hook.

"Ouch. That hurts."

"Sorry. But what's a little suffering, right?" He was applying thick liquid from three different pans with a paintbrush. "Nobody can do this the way I can. That's because, actually, I'm an artist."

"You are? You mean paintings and—"

"Mmm-hmm." He gestured. "That's one of mine."

Alice looked at the small framed watercolor next to the mirror. A bunch of grapes and a beach in the background.

She didn't know for sure if it was good or not. Anyway, she could tell it was grapes.

"It's nice," she said. "It's very nice."

"That was in Taormina. Notice the way the sunlight hits the purple? Have you been to Italy?"

"No."

"Great spot, Italy." He pulled another strand, and Alice winced. "I just moved into a new place and I want the walls exactly that color, grape purple. They're getting it all wrong. They gave me—eggplant! Can you imagine? It was a disaster. It'll take four coats at the very least. . . ."

He tied a cloth over her head and set a timer. Then Alice had to close her eyes, and he put cotton on the lids while he worked on her eyebrows and eyelashes.

"Don't move. . . . So, do you have a place to stay yet?"

"Oh, yes. I live in the city. I've always lived in the city." The stuff on her eyes felt funny. Damian's hand brushed against her cheek as he worked.

"That's good. You're all set then."

"Well," Alice said, "I'm planning to move. That is, if everything works out. . . ." She'd get a room to herself, with its own bathroom. And she'd forget about little blue-and-white-checked curtains like Rosie's. No, maybe she'd paint the walls purple. She'd never thought of dark walls before. Purple like . . . like a plum—that would be good. All white furniture, and maybe white irises in a vase . . .

"You'll work out, all right," Damian said. "When I get through, you'll stop traffic at the Cave."

"What's the Cave?"

"You're kidding. The Gilded Cave. Where've you been? *Everybody* goes to the Cave!"

"What is it? A disco?"

"You dance, don't you? You've *got* to make the Cave."

She felt him move in time to the Twisted Sister tape that was now pounding through the room. He left her while the coloring set. The chair was tilted back and her eyes were under cotton and she drifted into the music. She'd never even been to a disco. Her apartment was walking distance from the Salon and she'd lived in this same city all her life, but it seemed as if Damian inhabited another world. She'd like to be like Damian, bubbling and bopping around and talking about things she'd never heard of. Taormina—and what was Devonshire cream, anyway?

She smelled perfume and someone's cigarette smoke and a faint odor of ammonia.

Then she was rinsed off, and finally she could open her eyes again. She stared into the mirror. Her hair was too wet to tell what it would look like. Short hair made her neck seem longer. And her eyes were different. Drops of water ran down her neck and she shivered.

"This is the best part." Damian was back, with brushes and pencils and creams. "Now watch what I'm doing. I'm using a violet undertone to pale your skin. . . . This is *ivory* foundation. Blend it in like this. . . . Look at that, it makes your skin alabaster! That's what Renoir did, you know, color upon color, to get that radiance. . . . Now, white triangles at the outer corners of the eyes, extending to the temples, keep blending, you want to keep it subtle. It's an optical illusion, your eyes just go on and on forever. . . ."

Alice concentrated on each step. She'd have to remember how to do it. Her face was changing in bits and pieces; she focused on one spot at a time in the mirror as he worked.

"Beige shadow on the lids, carry it up to the eyebrows . . . dark gray in the crease, black liner . . . Start the liner in the middle, right here, we want to space your eyes. A dot, just a dot of yellow at the browbone, and more liner *under* the eye starting at the middle and extended way out. Smudge it a little—you don't want any hard, definite lines. It's all in the shading. . . . And gold highlighter. Pat it on above the crease and out to your hairline. . . . Keep blending. . . ."

Her eyes were enormous, and he was right, they did look amber, like tiger's eyes. They looked very made up, she'd never be able to go to school like that—but she loved it!

"Never put a whole row of lashes on. We don't want you looking like a hooker." He giggled, and Alice giggled, too, a little nervously. Was she all painted up like a hooker? "See, you take little tufts, just a few lashes, a little here, a little there, you don't need much, a tiny drop of surgical adhesive. . . . You'll get the hang of it, it takes practice. . . . So, what do you think?"

"I love it!" She looked a lot older and the eyes were *sexy!* She kept looking at them. "How did you do that, I look so . . ."

"I'm a genius," he said. Who had said that before? Oh, right, at the R&D, when they were talking about the guy who bonded teeth. He was a genius, too.

"They said I should have my canines shaved," Alice said. "Do you think I need my canines shaved?"

"It depends on the kind of look they want. No, don't worry

67

about it. You have a great smile. Iris could say things like that to keep you off balance, you know what I mean? Now, this is your basic makeup. You might add to it for different jobs or somebody else might do you differently, but this is what you should be aiming for. Now, a slightly darker foundation under the cheekbones to bring them out—use more if you're doing black-and-white—and the *slightest* touch of blusher under the eyes. . . . Brush it on *ever* so slightly, we don't want rosy and wholesome, keep it pale. . . ."

Alice stared and stared at her reflection. The bones were starkly defined. Her eyes stood out from the white, flawless skin. She looked harder, a lot harder—but terrific!

"Your lips are so good I'm almost tempted to leave them alone. Some transparent Terra Cotta, nothing heavy . . . . Follow your natural line with the brush, like this . . . and a *lot* of gloss."

He put mousse in her hair and brushed it and blew it dry. And all the way through, he talked and talked—about the makeover he had coming up in *Mademoiselle,* "Two pages, September issue, you'll have to catch it"; about the clever all-black dinner party his friend gave—caviar, Greek olives, pumpernickel, black bean soup, mussels, and a *sinful* chocolate soufflé, all on an *ebony* table; about some woman she'd never heard of, but obviously Somebody, who was caught in flagrante. In flagrante?

The sides of her hair were pushed straight back, close to her head. It was black, shining, shimmering.

"You want a clean line," Damian said.

The back was longer, cut at an angle to the nape of her

neck. He brushed the front straight up and left it there, somewhat wild, held up by the mousse.

"Voilà!"

She was finished, and Brett and some of the others crowded
around, smiling at her wide-eyed reaction, watching her.

". . . like a beautiful jungle animal, dangerous and devastating!"

"Superb!"

Alice saw Damian behind her reflection, grinning in
triumph. She was there somewhere, but transformed, sleek,
polished, grown-up. Alice laughed out loud, surprised, flushed
with pleasure.

9

After Damian's, Alice had to stop off at the agency. She walked fast, partly because it was near closing time and partly to keep pace with the excitement bubbling in her. She was aware of a new kind of attention from the people on the street. She liked it.

Alice went through the reception room and remembered how Bambi had cut a path through the crowd, drawing everyone's attention. Well, she wasn't walking like Bambi yet, but the receptionist said, "Hi," and Alice was sent straight through to Iris's office.

"Mmmm," Iris said. "Very nice. The little duckling is a swan."

Alice smiled, but she thought, the *ugly* duckling? She had been kind of pretty before, even if it was in a different way, hadn't she?

"Damian is just wonderful, isn't he? He exposed that long neck and that's a great asset, dear. Carry it proudly. Have you kept the diet?"

"Yes, I have." She would from now on.

"Good. The pounds should be dropping off. You're almost ready to be sent out. I know a lot of the girls make their rounds in jeans, but because of your age, dear, you have to be careful of your image. Something very polished, very good lines, fine quality. . . . You need to try for a certain sophistication. . . ."

"Oh. I don't have anything, really," Alice said softly, "except for jeans and . . ."

Alice saw the annoyance pass over Iris's face. "Well," Iris said, tap-tapping the pencil on her desk.

Even with the new haircut and makeup, Alice felt on the outside again.

A sigh. "I suppose it can't be helped. I'll have to order something for you." Iris jotted an address on a piece of paper and handed it to Alice. "Mona Designs. That's between Seventh and Eighth. They have a good line this year and they'll give us wholesale. Something black, I think. . . . I'll see. I'll order for you and we'll charge it against future earnings."

"Thank you, Miss Martin."

"Iris, dear. You're aware, of course, that I'm demonstrating enormous faith in your potential. Don't disappoint me."

"I won't. Thank you."

"All right. Stop by at Mona tomorrow. Now, check in with Billie and let's get you started."

Alice sat at the edge of Billie's desk, overwhelmed by the confusion of the booking room, while Billie alternately fielded

71

phone calls and jotted down the information that would go under Alice's picture in the agency catalogue: shoe size, dress size, height, weight.

Alice had weighed in at one twelve—three pounds off because she had barely eaten all weekend to make up for the Panagises' dinner.

"Of course, we can't put you on the headsheet until we have a photo. The first thing to do is start your go-sees and get your book together."

Billie kept mentioning the book—the all-important book, a zippered portfolio of at least ten good pictures.

The room was cramped, and Alice could hear the conversation at the next desk. Another model and her booker were hunched over a portfolio, sorting, rearranging, deliberating over the order of the photographs.

"I know it's not right," the model said. "Maybe the close-up in the hat should be first."

"Maybe. But it might have more impact after the big smiles."

"I don't know. Do you think so? *Something* blew my chances for that lipstick ad."

"All right. Let's try the hat in front. Then where do we position the profile?" They were intent on the pages as they slowly leafed through them.

"All that fuss over the order they're in?" Alice whispered to Billie.

"Everything counts," Billie said. "Your career depends on a really super book. It's your sales brochure. Most of the time, it's the book, not the model, that wins or loses a job. Okay,

I grant you, rearranging the pages gets to be an obsession with some of the girls, but you do want to get it just right."

"Oh."

"Here's your go-see list. And don't think you're the only girl in New York looking for test shots. Even though they're not for pay, you'll have to compete. When you land one and the shots are good, that means your book—and your career—is on its way."

"Not for pay," Alice echoed. She needed new shoes and all those cosmetics and . . . All of Jamie's pants were ridiculously short, he was growing so fast, but Claire said that could wait. First, they'd invest in Alice . . . but when would she start getting paid? And now she owed Iris for clothes. . . .

"You have to understand. It's an exchange of favors. The photographers need someone to test new equipment or a new idea. You need a variety of photographs—different styles, different moods. You need top-notch photographers to accentuate your strengths and teach you how to handle yourself in front of the camera."

Alice studied the go-see list. It was long, a lot of names, a lot of different addresses.

"What do I say? 'Hello, I'm a model'?"

"Introduce yourself, be sure to mention the Iris Martin Agency, explain that you need test shots. It's not that hard, Alice."

"Okay."

"Another thing. Since you're underage, you have the right to have a parent or guardian present at every shoot."

"My mother's working now and . . ." It was a good thing,

too, even if Jamie had to fend for himself in the afternoons.

"That's up to you and your mother. It's my obligation to tell you, that's all. Oh, and don't go to see John Alveira. He's on location now. Iris will call him personally and set something up for you when he gets back."

"Okay."

"So, go through the list. The big difference between the girls who make it and the girls who don't is just plain hustle."

"I'll hustle," Alice said.

Billie smiled. "I have a hunch you will."

When Alice came home, Claire and Jamie were already eating. Hamburgers and french fries.

"Oh, Alice!" Claire said. "You look so wonderful. Just like a model."

"Hi," Alice said. The smell of ketchup filled the kitchen. "Did you get dinner for me?"

"There's a burger in the pan. Help yourself."

"Hi, Alice," Jamie said.

"It's Monday! You know I'm supposed to have veal and asparagus tips on Mondays. I *gave* you the diet."

"I just came home from work and, anyway, *veal!* What's wrong with hamburgers? Oh, your hair, sweetie! It looks so different."

"I'm starving and you could at least have my dinner!"

"You don't have to come in here all upset without even—"

"I'm tired and I'm hungry!"

"—without even saying hello to anyone."

Alice sat down at the kitchen table, banging the chair legs against the floor. "All right. A burger. No bun. No fries."

Claire looked at her for a moment and then pushed herself out of her chair. "Okay, okay, no fries."

Alice scowled at the hamburger Claire served her. Her mouth was watering. It looked very small all alone on the plate. She drowned it in ketchup and ate quickly, with big bites.

Jamie was staring at her, studying her face.

"Tell us what happened," Claire said. "How did they get your eyes like that? I should do mine like that, too, right?"

"It's not for real life, Ma."

"I'll try it anyway. You know something? I could have been a model when I was your age. If I hadn't been stuck in Indiana and—" Claire lifted her hair up over her head.

"No, you couldn't, Ma."

"What?"

Alice felt hollow with hunger. "You don't have the cheekbones, Ma."

"How would you know what I had or didn't have?"

"All right. All right. Forget it."

"You're getting a swelled head, Alice. Veal and asparagus tips! Miss Prima Donna."

"I'm no prima donna! I'm just trying to—"

"You are so!" Jamie burst out. "A prima! I *hate* the way you look!"

"Come on, Jamie," Alice said. "What are you yelling about?"

"You look different." His lower lip was trembling.

"It all washes off," Alice said wearily.

"You look like a witch! And your hair stinks!" he said.

"Thanks a lot. Thanks a whole lot for making me feel so good."

"And you said . . ." His voice was quivering. ". . . you said you'd do something with me this afternoon. Something special."

"What? When?"

"Remember, on the phone, when you slept over Rosie's? You said."

"I didn't say today. I said some afternoon soon."

"I waited for you."

"Well, you shouldn't have."

"That's kind of mean, Alice," Claire said. "He expected you to—"

"I had to go to Damian's. I told you, Ma."

"You look mean," Jamie said.

Alice picked up a french fry from his plate and nibbled on it. "Tell you what. We'll do something good, real soon."

"Tomorrow? After school?"

"No, I can't."

"The day after?"

"I don't know. Soon." She caught the distrust on his face. "Jamie, listen to me. I have a lot to do. I have appointments to keep and clothes to pick up and—I can't promise a definite afternoon right now." She unconsciously took another fry from his plate. "Jamie, if I make a whole lot of money, the very first thing I'll do is buy you something. Okay? What do you want? If we're rich?"

"A bike! A blue ten-speed Schwinn." He said it fast, a well-rehearsed dream.

"You've got it. That'll be the first thing, I promise. So remember, if I'm busy and trying to get work, it's for your bike. And we'll still do things together when I have time." He looked satisfied and Alice didn't understand why she felt so close to tears herself.

"Everything's changing," she said, "but I'm not different. I'm not."

10

"Hey, Alice!" It was Rosie at the end of the hall. "Wait up!"

"Oh, Rosie, hi." Alice was at the school's front entrance, one hand poised to push open the heavy door.

"I have so much to tell you!" Rosie was next to her now, a little out of breath. "You won't even believe what happened to me! Mike gave me these diamond earrings—little studs, you know?—and my father hit the roof! He wants me to give them back!"

"He does? Why?"

"You know what my father said? What did I *do* to get diamonds! Is that crazy or is that crazy?" She lowered her voice as some other kids passed by. "And I have something else to tell you. Let's go to lunch and talk by ourselves. Come on, we have to talk."

"God, I wish I could," Alice said. She shifted her books and scraped her sneaker against the floor. "I've got to change and get my makeup on and—"

"Yeah, but what about lunch? I mean, you gotta eat."

"I'm supposed to have broiled fish and watercress salad. Now where am I supposed to get that?" Alice could smell the distinctive odor coming from the cafeteria, a combination of frying oil and ketchup. It would be good to sit down with Rosie and gossip like they used to. She'd been making the rounds all week and she deserved an afternoon off—but this afternoon, it wasn't just another go-see. Terry Gordon was seeing models for something specific.

"Come on, just for a little while. You've got to eat *something*."

"I have to rush. . . . I might grab a pretzel if the vendor's out."

"You're gonna get too skinny, Alice."

"No, because the camera adds ten pounds." Frank McCall had said she looked like a beanpole with the short hair. They didn't know, not even Rosie. And they hadn't seen her with makeup on and that made all the difference. "I've got to get moving."

"Yeah, okay . . . see you."

She sighed and pushed the door open.

Two weeks of skipping lunch, rushing, rushing through those precious few afternoon hours to make her rounds. . . . She tried to arrange the go-sees in some kind of geographical order, but she still wound up crisscrossing the city by bus and subway. The fares were adding up, too. The crosstown streets

79

were always jammed with trucks and sometimes it was faster to walk. West 20's, East 30's, one all the way up on 91st Street. She was driven to hurry, to squeeze one more go-see into the afternoon. "Hustle," Billie had said. Well, she was hustling, all right. Her new black pumps pinched. It was hard to feel fresh and confident at studio after studio.

She had hated that photographer on 91st Street. He had looked her over, not even returning her smile, and had said curtly, "You can leave a glossy."

"I don't have a picture yet."

"I suppose a slide will do," with annoyance.

"I don't have anything yet, but—"

"Then how do you expect me to remember you?" he had snarled.

Mostly, she'd wind up getting caught in the rush hour and by the time she came home, she was too tired to react when Jamie pounced on her. He was doing just about anything to get her attention. And it had been a mistake to promise him a bicycle.

"When, Alice? Tomorrow? Day after tomorrow?"

Now it was just one more thing she owed somebody.

In the evenings, Claire chattered and Alice tried to get some homework in. She did her nails and washed her hair and got her clothes ready for the next day.

Iris had ordered a black linen skirt and two linen tops, one white and one black, to alternate. Even at wholesale, she owed Iris a lot now. And the linen kept wrinkling, so Alice had to iron every night. She would put it off until the last thing at night and then finally make herself do it, knowing she had to and wanting to chuck the skirt and the modeling and just go to sleep.

Maybe today would be different. Billie had said Terry Gordon was a top photographer and did a lot of catalogues. This time, she wouldn't be going in cold. He was seeing models at two and maybe he'd choose Alice and . . . The pretzel vendor was out on the corner of Third Avenue, just as Alice had hoped he would be, and that could be a good omen. She bought a pretzel and ate it on her way home, enjoying the salty chewiness of the dough.

The bag lady was at her usual spot on First Avenue, bundled up in her layers even on this warm May day. Their eyes met and the bag lady extended her hand, fingers rounded, toward Alice, maybe toward the pretzel. Alice looked away quickly and walked faster. Iris Martin girls didn't have to worry about being out on the street, she told herself. Today she even had an *appointment*. If only she had her portfolio!

She hurried home and started on her makeup. She was getting better at it, even the eyelashes, getting it down to half an hour. Then she wriggled out of her sneakers and jeans and put on her working clothes. Her hair was last. She put on the Tenex and pushed up tufts of hair at the crown, the way Damian had shown her. The transformation was complete, and Alice looked at herself for a long minute, taking time to inhabit this new face. Sometimes, away from a mirror, she couldn't remember what she looked like.

Terry Gordon was on West 29th Street, way over near Ninth Avenue. She got off the subway and into the bustle of 34th Street at a little past one. She headed downtown, past a vendor with belts spread out on the sidewalk, "Check it out, check it out," past a cut-rate linen store, through the crowd in front of Penn Station, past a shabby old man who made kissing noises at her.

At 29th Street, the neighborhood changed abruptly. Store after store sold furs. Fun Furs. Goldman Fur Wholesalers. One window had small gray skins hanging. Then she was in front of Terry Gordon's building. She was too early. It would look dumb to show up that early. She'd been too nervous about being on time. Rush, rush, rush, and now she was stuck with almost an hour to kill. The high heels were painful. Maybe she could find someplace to sit and wait.

Alice walked a block east, past a parking lot. Faceless industrial buildings. A low, tan building with a neatly lettered sign, Fur Center Synagogue. It must be nice to belong somewhere, Alice thought. She wondered if there was a models' church; if there was, she'd join, even though she hadn't gone to church in years. A wiry black man rolled a rack of fur coats past her on the sidewalk, their luxurious brown sleeves bouncing slightly. Another block. She couldn't keep walking on those high heels for long; the balls of her feet hurt. Finally, on the corner, there was a luncheonette.

She sat down at the cracked white counter and ordered a cup of coffee. There were some men eating and talking at the far end, their clothes covered with fine white hairs.

"You want cream or sugar?" the counterman asked.

"No, black." Iris said no sugar, ever.

There was a big wall clock. One-twenty. Forty minutes to go. She sat at the counter and nursed the coffee and waited. A handful of customers came and went.

"Anything else?" the counterman asked.

"No, thanks."

The minute hand of the clock crawled too slowly around its circle. Her feet hurt and she felt an ache starting in her back.

The coffee was bitter. She didn't even like coffee.

The kids would be out of the cafeteria by now, Rosie and all of them, hanging out, talking, kidding around. Pretty soon, she wouldn't even know what was going on with them. She was suddenly filled with longing. What was she doing here anyway?

That clock hand wasn't moving.

She should have had soda. Her neck felt stiff and there was a bad taste in her mouth. The men at the far end were looking at her. She hated sitting all by herself with no one to talk to.

Finally she went back to Terry Gordon's studio, fifteen minutes early, and found the sleek anteroom filled with other models. They looked up at her as she came in, not unpleasantly, some half-smiling, but with a certain measuring look, sizing up the competition. Alice sat down and looked around the room, feeling the same calculating expression must be on her face, too.

"He's been delayed," Terry Gordon's assistant said. "There's a problem on a shoot. Apologies to everyone."

They waited. There were framed covers on the walls: Bloomingdale's Christmas catalogue, *Mademoiselle*, A&S *Spirit!*, *Elle*.

Some of the girls were intimidatingly beautiful, others less so; some were in full makeup and hairdo, others were clean-faced with hair simply slicked back, trusting their portfolios to

83

speak for them. All had the same general planes in their faces, wide-set eyes, small noses, definite chins, the special qualities that would work for a camera and be effective on a two-dimensional sheet of paper.

Alice wondered which ones were other Iris Martin girls. She wished she knew someone. She listened to bits of conversation.

". . . they had a specific look in mind. It was really a matter of them picking what they needed. I mean, it's not rejection, actually. . . ."

"Of course not, you can't take it personally. . . ."

Alice would take it personally, she knew she would. She needed to be chosen, to prove that Iris hadn't made a mistake. She waited, thinking and hoping, wishing there was something she could do to make Terry Gordon pick her. Success depended on the centimeters of her nose, the curve of her lips, a fraction of an inch more here, less there. It had nothing to do with anything she was or did. Becoming a model depended on plain physical luck.

". . . and do you know what that tramp did? She told Alveira I had a sunburn, so he didn't call me and he used her instead!"

"One day, she's going to have something fall on her, you know what I mean?"

"Anyway, you know that guy she was seeing, the one at McCann? I hear he's trying to shake her. . . ."

"Maybe, but he threw an awful lot of jobs her way."

"The ugly little tramp."

Alice listened. Plain physical luck—and hustle. But all she could do now was sit and wait.

When Terry Gordon arrived, he scanned the room.

"Sorry, girls, I'm running so late. . . . If you want, you can leave a picture with my assistant. Sorry, I've got to do this fast." There was absolute silence as he slowly looked at their faces. "You, you—and the redhead in blue," he said.

His assistant thanked the others and shooed them out. Most of the girls left pictures. Alice never even had a chance to introduce herself to him.

At least, Billie had promised her one definite shoot. Iris was supposed to be setting it up with John Alveira. She was lucky to have that.

11

This was it, finally, a real shoot with John Alveira. Alice had made up carefully at home so she wouldn't get nervous about keeping him waiting. And she had everything in her bag that Billie told her to take along. She didn't know exactly what she was supposed to do, but Billie said he would tell her. Billie said she'd be fine.

John Alveira was on Mercer Street in Soho. She got out of the subway at Spring Street and she had no idea of where she was. All the narrow little streets had names—Prince, West Broadway, Broome, crisscrossing each other crazily—instead of numbers that followed each other sensibly, like uptown. She had to ask directions twice and she had gone a block the wrong way and she worried about being late.

She walked a block east. There were art galleries and industrial buildings and a clothing store.

Another block with cobblestones, crowded with cars parked halfway on the sidewalk. A dusty bookstore. Soho was mostly old, but it was interesting.

She passed a restaurant and the smell enveloped her—garlic, basil, oregano. A sign in the window said Fresh Scungilli. She was so hungry. She'd had a tiny bit of salad for lunch and didn't even stop for a candy bar. She wanted to be just the right weight for this session.

Here it was—Mercer. Alice looked for numbers on the ancient buildings. Number ten. John Alveira's. Alice rang the bell beside a freight elevator. Billie had said she'd be fine. Billie would know, she told herself.

John Alveira had spent the morning in the darkroom in his underwear, checking yesterday's roll. A contact sheet of a one-dimensional face. He marked the best shots with a red grease pencil. Wind-machine–blown hair, sparkling with a thousand lights, more alive than the eyes. Not great. Good enough. John Alveira, shampoo salesman.

He pulled on jeans and a T-shirt and ran a comb through his hair. His throat was sore. Too many cigarettes, too much booze, a sleepless night, a cold coming on—no, he was playing games. He knew he was dreading the session coming up, dreading and anticipating and trying to squelch that irrational little stirring of hope.

He screwed the new lens onto the camera and cleaned old coffee cups out of the studio. Why the hell was he doing this? Why had he ever agreed to do test shots of what's-her-name? Well, to try out the new lens, right? Or because he owed Iris Martin a favor? No, my friend, he thought, cut the crap. He couldn't resist seeing the girl Iris had called a baby Magdalena.

She rang downstairs and he put out the twentieth cigarette of the day. He buzzed back and listened to the creak of the elevator.

She rang again at the entrance to the studio and he unbolted the heavy steel door.

"Hello. I'm—uh—Alice Lonner. I'm supposed to see Mr. Alveira?" She had a set little smile, trembling lips.

"Yes, yes, I'm John Alveira. Come in." He didn't know he had been holding his breath until he let it go.

There was a superficial resemblance, all right, the stark cheekbones, the large almond-shaped eyes—wrong color, though—and something about the nose, but that was it. Another beautiful plastic face, makeup by—most probably Damian. What in God's name had he expected?

He watched the girl walk awkwardly into the room. She held her arms tight against her sides. Not exactly the moves of a goddess.

"Please put your bag down anywhere." He made an effort to be pleasant. "So—you just signed with Iris?"

"Yeah—uh—yes."

Great. Personality plus.

"I have a change of clothing with me for—"

"No, that won't be necessary," he said.

"—for variety."

"No, I'll be taking mostly head shots. I'm going to use this." He draped the starched cotton-lace shawl around her shoulders. They were hunched with tension. God, she was wooden. Well, he'd make use of this session, play with textures. The crisp lace against soft skin, luminous eyes—her eyes, under the heavy shading and false eyelashes, looked like those of a panicked small animal. Was Iris getting senile or what?

"Your makeup looks okay. Unless you want to touch up?"

"Not if you think it's okay."

"It's good. Damian?"

"Yes. How did you know?"

"We might as well get started then." He pulled a white umbrella-shaded light out of the corner and plugged it in. "Have you been in New York long?"

"Yes," she said. "I mean, I live here."

"Mmm-hmm. Let's start with you here. Look past me, toward the window. More to your left."

"Like this?"

"Chin up. Not that much, just a little."

He watched her through the viewfinder as she tilted her head, stiffly following his instructions. She was obviously green. He knew he should be giving her a line of patter, something to put her at ease, but he didn't have the patience. He liked working with pros; he had cut his teeth with the greatest pro of them all.

"Pull the lace up to your lips. That's it." Click. What was her name again? "Agnes, give me a nice, sexy pout, okay?" Click. "Hold it." Her skin was soft and young. When he met Maggie, the lines around her eyes were beginning to show. That husky Southern-accented voice: "Are you going to *air-brush* the character out of my face, baby?" Maggie's eyes were alive, green fire.

"Uh—do you still want me to hold it?"

"What? No. Relax." He saw the strain in her neck. "Turn away from me and look at me over your shoulder. Part your lips." Click. "Come on, give me a look. Think Robert Redford." Click.

This girl was doing some kind of sexpot caricature, dumb, dull. Her resemblance to Maggie was offensive. An insult. He furiously readjusted the lights. He wanted to cut this short.

Alice could tell from the beginning that he didn't like her. The way he looked at her when she came through the door, not even bothering to hide his disappointment. And then he hardly said a word to her, just barking instructions.

She needed these shots to turn out good and John Alveira wasn't helping her at all, she knew that much. And Iris had said he would love her. "Turn." Click. "To the left." Click. "Hold it." Her neck was angled a funny way when he said that—and she held it and held it, concentrating on not moving, not moving a muscle, until it really started to hurt—and then he'd forgotten all about it! He made her feel stupid. Now her neck was aching, and the hunger was on the verge of turning into nausea. She wished she was someplace else—running down the street and laughing with Rosie, even just scrunched over the table playing Monopoly with Jamie. This was awful.

"Part your lips." Click.

He'd be good-looking for an older guy, if he didn't look so mean and angry. She hadn't done anything. She was trying so hard, and he made her feel that everything was her fault.

"Think Robert Redford," he said. What was she supposed

to do? She guessed he meant look sexy. She tried to pretend she was a centerfold in one of those magazines.

"Like this?" Alice said.

"Fine, fine, wonderful." He sounded so damn sarcastic. He was worse than any of them, worse even than that Wayne Hannigan at the R&D.

She had to make him like her.

"Take a break," he said. "I'm going to try something else."

He was fiddling with the camera and changing lenses. He almost slammed things around.

They said she had the right to bring a parent to a session, being underage and all. She almost wished Claire was with her. It felt so lonely all alone. If Mr. Panagis were here, if she were Mr. Panagis's daughter, he'd know what to do. He wouldn't let anyone treat her like some bimbo. Even Claire would at least make conversation. If only she could think of something to say to him, get friendly, make him like her.

"Mr. Alveira," Alice said.

"John is okay."

Alice took a breath and plunged in. "I saw your picture . . ." Should she have said *photograph?* ". . . the one of Magdalena? Iris has it in her office. It's really good."

He looked at her coldly.

"I liked it a lot. Magdalena was really beautiful, wasn't she?"

"Mmmm."

"I'd love to see her in person. I'm supposed to look like her. That's what they said when they discovered me."

His head was bent over the camera.

"Do I? I mean, do you think I do?"

He whirled toward her. "Fat chance! Magdalena was one of a kind!" His voice was ice, cutting her. He looked at her like she was some kind of insect to be squashed on the floor. "Let's get on with this. See if you can manage to smile."

Who the hell did he think he was? She'd had enough, enough of being hungry and getting a stiff neck and trying so hard!

"I never said I looked like her, *they* did. I don't know who she was and I don't care and I don't even want to be doing this!" Alice could feel her heart pumping. "I don't know what your problem is, mister. I'm Alice, not Agnes, *Alice* Lonner and—" She caught her breath with a gasp. "—and I don't want to be any damn Magdalena! Just because you're some big-shot photographer, you think you can—you think you can—"

She felt the tears starting and running down her cheeks. She was mortified. "And don't think you made me cry! I'm crying 'cause I'm mad, that's why!" She dropped the shawl and groped for the bag she had left on the floor.

He looked surprised. "Hey, wait a minute—"

"I quit. I've just quit." She wiped the tears roughly with the back of her hand and then realized that was a mistake. She had forgotten about her eyelashes and mascara. She wanted desperately to get through that doorway and disappear. Her eyes were smarting.

He blocked her way and he was actually smiling. "Wait a minute. You can't leave like this. Your eyelashes are hanging on your cheek."

She tried to push past him. He was laughing at her!

"No, really, wait."

"Let me go!"

"Look, I had a bad day, nothing personal." He led her away from the doorway. He tore a paper towel from a roll on the counter and handed it to her. "You're right, I'm wrong. Here, do something with this."

"I can't. I can't see what I'm doing."

"I don't usually eat models for breakfast. I'm a nice guy, I swear. There's the bathroom; go wash your face."

She hesitated. He confused her and made her feel ridiculous.

"Go on," he said.

She ran blindly into the bathroom and slammed the door behind her, glad to get away from him. Now he'd go and tell Iris that she was no good. She sniffled and looked at herself in the mirror over the sink. She looked like a damn raccoon! A tuft of lash was stuck to her cheekbone. She made a little packet of the paper towel, carefully removed the eyelashes, and put them in. She might as well save them, just in case. She found a box of tissues and blew her nose.

She heard him call to her through the door. "Someday, you'll think this is funny."

"Yeah, you're a real comedian!" she yelled back. Loser!

He sure kept a messy bathroom. There was a pileup of wet towels hanging over the shower rod and a hamper in the corner with things spilling out. And the floor wasn't too clean either. She hated him and she didn't even want to use his soap, but she scrubbed her face clean with it and dried it with more tissues. Her hair was wet and she slicked it straight back. In the mirror, she was back to regular Alice Lonner again and that was okay. In a way, she was glad it was all over.

She didn't want to look at him when she came back into the studio, but she forced her head up and looked him right in the eyes. She wasn't going to crawl out of there.

He was staring at her, an odd look on his face.

"Where did you put my bag?"

He didn't answer for a long minute, staring at her. "Christ!" he said. "Exactly how old *are* you?"

"Look, mister, I want my bag." She wasn't about to leave without it, not with all that expensive makeup and—

"I said, how old are you?"

"Fourteen. And what's that got to do with the price of tea in China?" She saw the bag on the counter and brushed by him to pick it up.

"Nobody likes a smart-ass." He was smiling. "Fourteen. I didn't know."

"So what?"

"Listen—uh—Alice. We're going to start from the beginning. I'll get some shots of you just like this—Jesus, a fourteen-year-old kid—and then—"

"Iris doesn't want pictures of me without makeup. I'm supposed to be high fashion."

"A high-fashion exotic, right?" He started laughing.

"Yeah, and what's so funny?"

"You're right, it's not funny. I can see what Iris had in mind. I'll take a few like this and then you can get your makeup on and—"

"No. I don't want to."

"Hey, don't let it be said that John Alveira deprived the world of another exotic."

"No. Forget it." He was being sarcastic again!

"Now you sound like a twelve-year-old. You're regressing fast."

"Anyway, it takes me a long time."

"I've got time."

Alice hesitated. She should be glad he was giving her another chance. What would Iris say or Claire or the kids at school?

"Look, I owe you one," he said. "I'm not a total lowlife."

"You could've fooled me."

He laughed again. "In lieu of apology, the great Alveira is going to set you up with a dynamite portfolio." He stuck out his hand. "Friends?"

Alice shrugged and shook his hand. That was something Jamie would do, shake hands to make up and say "friends."

"Stay mad," he said.

"What?"

"You were too uptight before. Now you're giving off energy."

"Well, it was my first shoot. What did you expect?"

"Okay."

"And besides, all I ate all day was a couple of celery sticks!"

"Anorexia city. The famous Iris Martin diet."

"You know about it?"

"Do you want something to eat?"

"I'm not supposed to—between meals—"

"Screw the Iris Martin diet. I'll scare up a sandwich." He led her around a tall screen and into another large space. In the corner, there was an unmade bed with a mound of wrinkled sheets. Light streamed in through huge leaded windows. Kitchen equipment hugged a wall, fronted by a butcher-block table and chairs.

Alice wondered if *her* apartment would look better if all the walls were knocked down—but then it wasn't as large as this and didn't have a nice, pale wood floor to reflect the light. And there'd be nothing to separate her from Claire and Jamie.

"A photographer's supposed to know how to turn his model on," he said. "Robert Redford was my mistake. I should have said 'double-scoop ice cream sundae.' "

Alice laughed.

"And you can smile. Terrific."

"You could have said Tom Cruise."

"I see we've got a generation gap here."

Alice was getting to like him, in spite of herself. There was something down-to-earth real about him, and he was very attractive for an older guy.

John leaned against the table and watched Alice devour the cheese and tomato sandwich he had made for her. She seemed to be trying for daintiness—the way she placed the napkin on her lap, the way she carefully picked up the sandwich half— but then she shoveled the food in with huge bites. He took a shot of her, cheeks puffed with food, eyes still wary.

"Don't do that," she said. "Why are you taking me like this?"

"Don't pay any attention," John said. "It's like a nervous tic with me."

He had no particular plan in mind. After the first shock of seeing her—Christ, she looked like a little urchin!—he was amused by the contrast and idly thought he'd get it down on paper. Now he was feeling some kind of urgency. The curve of her chin was vulnerable and childlike, and now the starkness of the high cheekbones, stripped of makeup, made her look touching, deprived somehow.

"You want something to drink? Milk or something?"

She screwed up her nose. "I hate milk. Anyway, it's fattening."

"Soda?" The refrigerator was amost empty—half a tomato, a six-pack, the remains of a salami.

"Is it no-cal?"

"What? No, regular Pepsi."

"Oh. Well, then I can't," she said mournfully.

"Go ahead. Live a little." He poured a glass.

"Thanks a lot. I mean it. I'm sorry I was so—so unprofessional before."

"It's okay. You don't have to let anyone push you around."

"So you'll give me another chance? Take more pictures, with makeup and everything?"

"I promised I'd give you something good for your portfolio, didn't I?"

How could he have thought she was blank? Her eyes expressed everything; they were achingly hopeful. Earlier, when she had allowed her anger to show, they were blazing. He remembered the face, the snarl, the fury just before the tears came. A tough little street kid. Iris was right about her. With proper handling, she could be a top-notch exotic. If he kept her relaxed, if she was responsive to the camera, those bones could carry an image of raw sexuality. . . . Christ, he thought. The ultimate woman—a fourteen-year-old!

"How did you get involved with Iris?" he asked.

He listened to pieces of her story. At ease, she was talkative between bites and sips. Something about Pat Richards and shopping bags, graphic art and high school.

"You like art?"

"I do, a lot! My class went to this museum once, the Whitney, and—" Her face was animated. "—and there was this painting that looked so *happy*. . . ."

Her smile was wonderful, somewhat wistful, a child looking at a Christmas window. Maybe he'd take her to a museum, see if he could capture more of that expression. . . . What was he thinking of? Why? And it came to him all at once. What a series it would make! Photograph her both ways. The illusion of a woman's sexuality, created, like a female impersonator's, out of eyelashes, lighting, fashion. And then this child—too thin, defensive, innocent, exploited for the tenderness of her unlined flesh. He should have gotten a shot of her crying, with the clownlike disarray of makeup; well, he'd create other opportunities. He wanted to get to work!

"Are you finished?" he said. "Let's do it. Use more shadow. Exaggerate your eyes. . . ." He would parody Magdalena's look—the sultry ethnic. (Maggie used to laugh at herself, used to do her femme fatale takeoff at parties.)

He watched her reluctantly put down the last bread crust, pick up her bag, and head toward the bathroom.

"I'll try not to be too long," she said over her shoulder.

"No, no, take your time." He couldn't show impatience. He had to keep her relaxed. "Tell you what. When we're through, I'll take you over to Ferrara's."

"Ferrara's?"

"The best cannolis in the city."

He was rewarded with wide-open shining eyes.

Something worthwhile was going to come out of this deadly day, with its freshly raked up memories of Magdalena. With Maggie as his mentor, he had become stuck in her world, too successful to get out. Well, Maggie had gotten out in her own way.

"I'm tired of worrying over every little line," she had said. "I just want to let go. . . ."

He heard she was happy. Married to her bald, indulgent count, living in an ancient villa in Tuscany, getting fat and lazy, the glorious face still intact. She had had so much iron discipline for so long. And she had done him a favor by introducing him to the right people, posing for him, starting him on a too-early skyrocketing career. . . .

With Alice Lonner, maybe John Alveira still had something to say. How much pressure could she handle? Was she going to crack? "Children under Stress." Or "Children of Strife." He'd use other subjects, too, but this girl would be the centerpiece. It could be one hell of an exhibit! If he could get it on film . . .

Later, he showed Alice how the lights were hitting the planes of her face. He talked her through it, he babied her, he turned on mood music, he freed her to fantasize, he taught her to make love to the camera. "Beautiful. That's beautiful, Alice."

Click. "Great. Wonderful." Click. Her face was mobile and expressive putty. He'd get her editorial work, take her in a luxury wardrobe to juxtapose against the waif gulping down a soda. "Terrific. More, give me more. You're a natural." Click. "That's super." He felt saddened by how eagerly she responded to every bit of approval. She seemed willing to work until she dropped.

Anyway, he was giving her excellent material for her portfolio. Iris would love it.

12

Alice glanced sideways at John. His eyes were startlingly blue against his dark coloring. Walking with him was comfortable; his stride matched hers, he was just tall enough, his arm held hers with exactly the right amount of pressure to maneuver her through the kaleidoscope of people and stores on Grand Street.

"You'll love Ferrara's," he said.

"This is awfully nice of you," she said. "You don't have to—"

"We've got to celebrate your debut." His smile flashed bright white against olive skin. He was so nice and relaxed now; their awful beginning seemed like eons ago.

They were walking on a block where the edges of Chinatown rubbed against Little Italy. Chinese lettering, a Chinese grocery, Italian restaurants with freshly set tables and heady smells floating out into the narrow, crowded street. Ferrara's sign twinkled with little light bulbs. Alice looked in the large glass windows that flanked the entrance. There were three fantastic wedding cakes, tier upon tier upon tier, outdoing each other in height and in elaborate gossamer details. One had a double flight of spun-sugar stairs curving down from the highest tier, populated by an entire wedding party.

"Wow, that's beautiful!"

He laughed. "It's a little much."

"Oh, no! I think it's—" She swallowed her words. She didn't want to sound so easily impressed.

It was almost twilight. The air had chilled and there was a soft blue haze over the street. Inside, the brown-and-white-tiled room exploded with brightness, warmth, and the buzz of conversation. A long bakery counter displaying an incredible assortment of pastries ran the length of one side. Through the crush of customers, she saw a mouth-watering variety—rows of whipped cream, flaked chocolate, candied confetti, colored icing, cherry toppings, custard creams, glazed brown shells in many shapes.

"I'll never decide. . . ." she said.

They went to the less crowded upstairs section and sat at a table. She studied the menu and listened to John weigh the virtues of mille foglia over baba au rhum, or perhaps they should have cannolis or torta di ricotta. . . . She laughed at how serious and intense he was. He didn't seem that much older anymore.

"Don't laugh," he said. "This deserves careful consideration."

"You really do have a sweet tooth, don't you?"

"Well, yes, but I was thinking—if you're going to break Iris's rules, it should be memorable."

"Oh, why did you remind me!"

"I was kidding, Alice. Don't feel so guilty."

"But Iris said a few more pounds would—"

"You're just about perfect; I'd be the first to tell you if you weren't."

"You think I'm perfect?" she said warily. No one had ever said quite that to her.

He grinned. "Only physically, my dear. I don't know about the dark spots on your soul."

He was teasing, but he made her feel perfect, she thought. When she was posing for him, his words had spun a magical glow about her and she could do no wrong. That beautiful feeling had stayed with her; she liked seeing herself in his eyes. She loved being with him!

They had settled on mille foglia, leaves of pastry separated by creamy custard and topped with bright red icing, and cups of foamy cappuccino. He ate with concentrated enjoyment.

"Did I steer you right? Is this great?"

A family group sat down at a table near them. The obvious head of the family was a somewhat heavy, very dignified gentleman, thickly mustached and impeccably suited. There were women of various ages and a number of children, squirming in best suits or dresses, on good behavior under the watchful eyes of the patriarch. Alice watched wistfully as they ordered and argued and wriggled. It would be nice if she and Jamie had a regular afternoon excursion for pastry, but just the two of them—or even three, with Claire—wasn't enough.

He followed her glance to the neighboring table. "They look nice, don't they?"

"I'd imagine you like—like that little boy." A bright-eyed five-year-old, secure in his place, was stealing whipped cream from his mother's plate.

"No. My father was a fisherman, a first-generation immigrant. There was an accident; he died at sea. It was hard-scrabble after that."

"I don't have a father, either," Alice said.

"Oh?"

"I have my mother and my little brother, Jamie. He's seven. . . . Were you poor?"

"Yes. Well, I guess everything's relative. I never went hungry—but I can't get my fill of pastries."

There was a common chord between them, Alice thought. He wasn't from another world like Iris or Wayne Hannigan or Damian. Well, not all the time.

"But you seem—so suave and—I don't know." She stopped, embarrassed at having said too much. Her defenses were way down, partly because she was tired. Mostly, because of him. He was so interested in everything she had to say.

"I'm a long way from New Bedford."

"How did you—?"

"I got a Brownie camera for Christmas the year I was nine. I took to it right away. There was a big fire at one of the piers and I happened to be there. I took a lot of shots—before I turned in the alarm. Well, somebody else turned it in, actually. That's the photographer's quandary, you know—do you record the disaster or do you try to help? Anyway, the local paper used my shots and that was pretty heady for a kid. I knew exactly what I wanted after that."

"Would you do that? Take pictures and not try to help at all?"

"I didn't say not help at all. Yes, I'd help, but I'd sure try to get the picture first. You're psyched to go for your camera and there's that one perfect split-second image you don't want to lose. I don't know; that's theoretical. I guess it depends on the disaster."

"How did you become a big-shot fashion photographer?"

She watched the warmth go out of his face. "It's a long story," he said.

"What happened?"

"I was in a fashion photography class at Parsons. That wasn't my real interest; we all took a variety of classes and— It seemed Magdalena had worked with one of the instructors and she came as a guest lecturer, from a model's point of view. She was a legend. And I was twenty years old and impressionable, and we talked after class. I took some shots of her, and she introduced me to a lot of people. So I quit school and kind of fell into a career." He sipped his cappuccino and looked into the distance.

"Magdalena. That sounds so exotic," Alice said.

"Maggie MacIver of Athens, Georgia. I'm surprised Iris didn't rename you. Alicia, at least."

Alice shrugged. "It's not like anyone knows my name."

"Oh, but they will."

"Do you really think so?" she asked him in wonder.

"I know so. And I'd like to hang around and watch it happening to you."

Alice felt a delicious little shiver run through her body. He was so sure it would happen. Even if he seemed so regular now, she had to remember he was a top photographer and he would know. And he wanted to hang out with her! He wasn't coming on to her or anything, he was just nice and he seemed to really like her! Her world was changing in one afternoon.

She hesitated. "Do I remind you of Magdalena? Is that why?"

"No, you don't," he said. "Maybe there's a resemblance for someone else to see, but . . . When I was a kid, there were identical twins that lived down the street from us. I was best friends with one of them. Frankie. No one else could tell them apart. To me, they didn't even look alike. When you know someone very well . . ."

"I understand," Alice said. He was interested in her for herself, not because of some resemblance—that's what he meant, wasn't it? Billie had said something about John Alveira and Magdalena living together, but that was long ago. . . .

"Well, enough about me," he said. "Let's talk about why *you* like my photographs."

"What?"

"A joke. No, I want to hear about you. Tell me about your family and your school and—"

He listened attentively as she talked. He seemed interested in every detail.

She hated having him call for the check. She wanted to

spend more time with him. She had a feeling the sweet taste of custard and pastry leaves would always be part of a special longing.

"How old are you?" she said.

"Thirty-one. Why?"

"I just wondered."

He laughed. "Because of the childlike way I wolf down whipped cream? Now you know my secret vice."

He wasn't *that* old. He was awfully attractive—straight nose, those startlingly blue eyes, an amused expression that made him seem to have seen it all. And the intense way he looked at her was exciting.

On the way out, he put his arm around her waist as he guided her past the crowd at the bakery counter. She felt his hand through her linen blouse.

It didn't matter that he was a lot older, she thought. After all, she was a high-fashion exotic, wasn't she?

13

Iris and Billie saw the proofs from John Alveira before Alice did, and they selected the shots they would use without even asking what Alice thought.

"Iris was very happy," Billie said, when she finally handed them over to Alice one day in the booking room. "We'll use this one for the headsheet." It was a shot of Alice looking directly into the camera, lips parted, nostrils slightly flared, eyes arrogant. It looked like a *model*, it looked like one of those sexy starlets on TV commercials, it looked like someone who'd been everywhere and done everything. She didn't know she could look like that. Had John Alveira done tricks with lighting or was it the terrific, confident way he made her feel? She couldn't remember what she had been thinking when it was taken.

"We'll put that and the profile into your portfolio. And maybe this one, too. They're wonderful, but John Alveira can't be your *whole* book." Billie glanced curiously at Alice. "He certainly took a lot of time. That must have been quite a session."

Alice studied the three black-and-white sheets: Alice smiling, Alice pouting, in profile, three-quarter view, eyes wide open, eyes half-closed like a sleepy cat. For the first time, all the things Iris and the others had been saying made sense; there was something about her bone structure that allowed a camera to create this glamorous, older, familiar stranger. She didn't know who she was; she wanted to look in a mirror.

"I look so different in each one," Alice said.

"Well, that's very good, dear," Billie said over her shoulder and continued her phone conversation.

John hadn't sent the other shots, the silly ones of her eating and talking without makeup, and she was glad. She didn't even want to see those. The good part was when she had posed for him. She had been bathed in a warm, buttery light and he kept saying "Terrific!" and there was absolutely nothing she couldn't do. When she thought about it afterward, that adored and super-powerful feeling seemed like a fantasy. But these shots were proof: she was spectacular. She liked being Her. And she couldn't wait to see John Alveira again.

"Look, I'm sorry," Billie was saying into the phone. "Her Wednesday afternoons are blocked out. . . . That's what she wants. Believe me, there's no point in pursuing it. . . . No, I can't do a thing. . . . Okay, talk to you later." She grimaced and replaced the receiver. "Go figure it. That was for Dena

McDonald—everyone wants her and *she* wants to be an actress, so she's giving up half her time for some stupid rehearsals, not even at scale, mind you! She's losing a fortune and Iris is furious."

"Why would she do that?" Alice asked.

"Search me. Anyway, Iris is high on you now and you're invited to her Connecticut place on Saturday."

"Me? On Saturday?"

"Every now and then, Iris invites her promising girls to her country home. This time, it'll be you and Kerstin and Jessica."

"This Saturday? I promised my little brother I'd—"

"Alice, this is a command performance—and you're to consider yourself honored."

"Okay, sure. . . ."

"It's a sign that she thinks you're *very* promising. And it is a lovely place."

"How do I get there?"

"Don't worry about that. She'll send a car."

Alice was ready and fidgeting by nine-thirty on Saturday. She had given Jamie breakfast and explained for the tenth time why she couldn't spend the day with him. He listened to her suspiciously.

"But why?"

"Because this is business." She hadn't put her makeup on. Iris said to give her skin a rest whenever she could and this would be daytime, in the country.

"What kind of business?" Jamie said.

"I don't know. Just business." She wore clean jeans and her

nice blue shirt. Jeans should be all right and she didn't have anything else, anyway.

"I'll go to the Emporium with you. I'll carry bags. I will."

"Forget that, Jamie."

"Why?"

"Leave me alone. I have to get ready." She decided to put her eyelashes on. She felt too naked without them. She added shadow. There, that was better. Now she looked more like the girl in the photographs.

When she came out of the bathroom, Claire was up, tying the belt of her old beige bathrobe.

"Are you ready to go?"

"Yes, just about."

"Don't you want to wear my good blouse?"

"No. This is okay, don't you think? It's just the country." Anyway, she'd learned that Claire's good things were overdone.

"Who's going to be there?"

"Some other models. I don't know."

"I bet it'll be an estate. I bet there'll be horses and— Wouldn't you think she'd invite your mother, too? If it's a party, after all."

"It's not a party." Alice felt a knot in her stomach.

"I bet there'll be a pool and a big buffet and—"

"I'd better go and wait out front," Alice said.

She stood in front of the building and saw everything vividly—the overflowing garbage cans, the graffiti on the front door, the rusting fire escape. She felt like she needed to go to the bathroom again.

A long black limousine pulled up in front of her. Alice

couldn't see into the back seat. The chauffeur, a lean black man in a gray uniform, got out and consulted a note in his hand.

"Alice Lonner?"

"Yes."

"I'm Kenneth." He opened the backseat door with a flourish and held it as she got in. She felt herself moving extra gracefully. She hoped the people on the street were noticing her.

"Hi. I'm Kerstin and this is Jessica," the blonde girl in the back seat said. She had an accent.

"Hi. I'm Alice Lonner." She sank deep into soft red leather upholstery and the door slammed shut.

"We know. Billie told us." Kerstin smiled. "You're brand new and Iris has invited you already. You're lucky."

"Some luck," Jessica said. She had short honey-brown hair and was wearing glasses. "Iris calls and we all have to jump! I've got a term paper due and my finals, and the last thing I need is to waste a day!"

"Ssshhh, he will hear you," Kerstin said.

"The partition is up—we can talk," Jessica said, "unless Iris has the back wired. I wouldn't be surprised."

Kerstin giggled. "Jessica is terribly intellectual and goes to Barnard. She's going to read the whole way up, so we will have to talk in tiny whispers."

"I give up. I can't study in a car, anyway." Jessica pushed the glasses up to her forehead and exposed huge hazel eyes.

Kerstin had long, pale blonde hair, porcelain skin, and deep blue eyes. Her mouth was full and pink and she had a delicate sculptured nose. She was as beautiful as anyone Alice had ever seen and she looked slightly familiar.

Jessica looked sturdier, with regular features and dimples that flashed in her cheeks when she spoke.

Alice was relieved to see that they were casually dressed, too—Jessica in jeans and a loose polo shirt, Kerstin in a full denim skirt and a white tank top that showed her round, firm breasts.

The car was gliding noiselessly along city streets.

"Have you been with Iris long?" Alice asked.

"It only seems like forever," Jessica said. "A couple of years, actually."

"I came to New York a year ago and it's been wonderful!"

"What, being with Iris?" Jessica looked skeptical.

"No, New York! It became wonderful when I moved out of Iris's." Kerstin turned to Alice. "I had to live with her at the beginning, can you imagine? I traveled to Copenhagen to see her, when she was scouting there, and when she signed me, my father said no. He wouldn't let me come! I would have gone, no matter what, because I come from a little place with pigs and chickens. Ugh!" She wrinkled her perfect nose. "So Iris said I could live with her and be *chaperoned*. It was crazy. But now I have my own place and everything is wonderful! I've been working all the time."

"You're from Denmark?" Alice asked.

"Yes, a little town in the north. You would never have heard of it."

"You speak English awfully well."

"Oh, we study English in school. And I did quite well with it because I always had the dream to go to Hollywood. But now models are like movie stars, aren't they?"

"You look familiar," Alice said.

113

"I had the cover of *Bride's* in March."

"Kerstin is our professional angel," Jessica said. "Anything that involves sugar and white lace—there's Kerstin."

"Like Baby Love perfume," Kerstin said. "And Heavenly Shine shampoo."

"I'm your standard healthy type," Jessica said. "All-American. I have a commercial where I swim and chew gum. And there's one where I do cartwheels because I test negative on dental cavities."

"Where are you from?"

"North Bay. That's the north shore of Long Island, not very far. I live at school now."

"Jessica says she hates modeling," Kerstin said. "I love it!"

"I don't *hate* it. It's a great way to pay my tuition. When my parents split up, I was short on cash and I waited tables at Moody's—you know, at 73rd Street?—and I was knocking myself out. Well, I met this photographer and he set up an appointment with Iris and the rest is history." Jessica shrugged. "I won't be doing this for long, though. Not after I graduate."

"I want to model forever!" Kerstin said.

"Great. What do you do when you hit thirty?"

"Oh, pooh. I don't know. I'll probably be married to a *very* rich man." Kerstin giggled again.

"How old are you?" Alice asked.

"Seventeen," Kerstin said.

"Twenty-one. On my last legs," Jessica said. "And you?"

"Fourteen."

"That's very young," Jessica said. She looked thoughtful. "Don't let yourself get overwhelmed."

Alice wanted to ask what she meant, but Jessica pushed her glasses over her eyes and said, "I've got to finish this chapter. Maybe I'll take the train back early."

"Iris won't like that," Kerstin said.

"Tough." Jessica turned a page and leaned over her thick textbook.

Jessica was all right, but Alice really liked Kerstin.

"Have you ever been there before?" Alice asked her. "What happens?"

"Sure, lots of times. What happens? Iris usually has a few other people and there's always Miles—he's very handsome, you'll see. And when we sit down to eat, Iris watches your manners like a hawk and instructs you. I didn't know anything, which little fork to use or spoon, and she embarrassed me! Just wait and imitate whatever she does; it's not hard. The trick is to use the silverware from the outside in. I was so ignorant! But I know all about the things that matter, more than Iris does." Kerstin laughed. "Oh, and then there's the discussion of the wine and the good years and she makes you pronounce the name—but she won't let any of us have more than a glass! Do you want a coke?"

"Okay."

Kerstin opened the bar compartment in the car. "Coke— meaning cola." She giggled. "She took out all the liquor before she sent the car for us. That's Iris. Sometime in the afternoon, she will lecture you about the Iris Martin image and all the things we mustn't do. It's funny. . . . Do you have a boy-friend?"

"No."

"Really? Not even part-time? Well, I know a million interesting men who'd *die* to meet you."

"Do you have a boyfriend?"

"Oh, yes. He's wonderful, but I hardly ever get to see him. He's at Annapolis. I did a fashion show and there were all those cute midshipmen lined up to escort us down the runway—it was a benefit, that's why, with the Annapolis chorus—and that's how I met him. He's so cute in that nice white suit—so pure and sheltered—and he writes to me almost every day. I'm quite sure I'm going to marry him. His name is Kevin. Isn't that sweet?"

They sipped diet colas and watched the highway stream past the window. Alice stretched her legs.

"We could watch television, if you wish."

"Oh, please!" Jessica looked up from her book and yawned. "Anyway, we're almost there."

They passed shorefront and trees budding in many shades of green. The car turned up a ramp and now the roads were narrow, with widely spaced houses.

"Her garden was featured in *Town and Country*," Kerstin said.

"Of course, you can guess what it featured," Jessica said.

Alice looked at her blankly.

"Why, beds of irises, of course."

"Oh, they were truly beautiful," Kerstin said. "White and purple. I think it's past the season for them now."

They turned into an entrance between high stone walls.

"This is it," Jessica said. "The country seat of the empire."

14

The maid ushered them past a terrace where Alice caught a glimpse of people and heard tinkling glasses. They were directed to the living room, a sea of red: red oriental carpets, red paisley couches, vivid paintings against red brick walls, a collection of red clay rabbits on a huge stone mantel, displays of mixed bouquets featuring red tulips.

"Country with a capital C," Jessica said.

Iris swept into the room, her wide silk pants swirling around her long, narrow legs. She greeted each of them with little kisses in the air, just missing their cheeks.

"You'll meet the others later," she said. "I thought we'd talk first, just *entre nous*. Sit down, girls. Alice, here," she said, patting a cushion. "It's so helpful to have an informal chat on a nice, relaxed day, especially for the new girls, don't you think?"

"Oh, yes," Kerstin said.

"And of course, I wanted you to meet Jessica and Kerstin. You'll find you'll learn most of what you need to know from the other girls—how to turn on a runway, how to remove a coat, things of that sort."

"I'll show her," Kerstin said. "You'll see, there's nothing to it. It just takes a bit of practice."

"That's why modeling schools are such a rip-off," Jessica said. "If you've got the look, you can pick up the rest."

"You do need some fine-tuning in terms of poise and self-confidence, dear," Iris said, "but don't worry, I'll see to it. My home exposes you to a certain environment, a certain level of sophistication. . . . In return, I expect you to uphold the tradition of the Iris Martin model. If Jessica and Kerstin have heard this before, well, it certainly can't hurt to hear it again."

"Right," Jessica said.

"Alice, you are part of our family now and I want my girls —" She interrupted herself with a disarming little smile. "—my *daughters* to be the very *best* they can be. Perfect body, perfect grooming, ladylike manners, that Iris Martin polish. I want you to work out regularly—Billie will give you a list of approved gyms. Follow the diet, have Damian maintain your hair *religiously*, take meticulous care of yourself, be punctual and courteous to all appointments, and live a *wholesome* life to keep your skin and eyes shining bright. I'm here to guide you and advise you and, yes, protect you. And I'm sure you'll work hard and do very well."

"Oh, I'll try!" Alice said.

"And on the subject of working hard, Jessica. I hear you've asked to be blocked out for two weeks?"

"For my finals," Jessica said.

"DMB&B specifically requested you for that deodorant commercial and you're blocked out! Did you expect them to *wait* for you?"

"No, but—"

"So another agency got it! Do you know what we've lost in billing?"

"I'm sorry, Iris, I need the time to study for—"

"You could work around it."

"I can't. I'm taking a pre-engineering class; it's hard and —"

"Engineering? Whatever for?"

"Well, I want to be an architect, so—"

"And for that, you'd jeopardize your modeling career? Think, Jessica! You can make a perfect edifice of yourself. Isn't that more meaningful than some brick building?"

"I think I prefer an edifice where someone's home upstairs."

"You've got an attitude, Jessica. Just remember where we found you. Just remember who you were."

"And you picked me up out of the gutter! Come on! I was a college student, Iris, and I was waitressing."

They stared hard, unblinking, at each other. Jessica broke first.

"I've never missed a scheduled shoot and you know the photographers like me. All I'm doing is taking a little time off and then I'll be free all summer."

"Don't ever let anything like this happen again. That's all. And speaking of an amateur attitude, that's something I want to discuss with you, Kerstin."

"What did *I* do? I'm always available."

"Oh yes, available indeed!"

"What's the matter, Iris?"

"Harry Wainwright called to complain. You were a zombie on that last shoot."

"Oh, that! It was just that one time. I took a Valium and I didn't know it would—"

"And you're getting a reputation for unreliability. When your night life starts to interfere, Kerstin—"

"But—"

"If you close every disco, don't think it won't show on your face. When you lose the fresh look, you're through."

"But Iris—"

"You understand me. . . . Oh, I do want you to teach Alice the pirouette. We might try you on runway, Alice, for the fall shows. . . . Now come meet the others. Lunch is about to be served."

Iris led the way to the adjoining terrace and made the introductions. Renata was about forty, with chipmunk cheeks and sharp little black eyes. Helaine was older, very thin and bony, with too small, unbelievably perfect teeth. Raoul, in his twenties, was wiry and nervous-looking. Miles had perfectly groomed dark hair, chiseled features, and the smoothest, most even tan Alice had ever seen. His muscular chest tapered sharply to a narrow waist and slim hips.

On the way into the dining room, Iris put one arm around Helaine and the other around Alice. "She's brand-new, just hatched. John Alveira took some marvelous shots. I'll send them over to you, darling, before anyone else gets a crack at her. . . ."

The dining room table was set like a magazine illustration, Alice thought. There was a floor-length starchy white tablecloth partly covered by a pale yellow square. The napkins were yellow and white bandannas. Sprays of daffodils and little white china rabbits ran the length of the table. The silverware had handles of gold and there were crystal wine glasses and goblets and . . . and . . . Alice had never seen anything like it.

There was a hubbub of conversation and the maid served the first course. Alice looked at the shell-shaped plate in front of her. It was edged with gold and contained two tiny curled-up shrimp on a lettuce leaf. She knew enough to use the little fork at the outside of the elaborate place setting. Iris watched her and smiled.

"Raoul," Renata said. "Your ideas this season were stunning."

"Absolutely original," Helaine agreed.

Alice's shrimp went down with two fast gulps. Maybe first courses were supposed to be very small.

"I see the East Village kids wearing those torn T-shirts, Fruit of the Loom, you know?" Raoul said. "So I get a shipment of tees and cut them here and there, each one different, man, the way the inspiration hits me—it's a rush, you know?—and then nailheads go around each hole, artistically, you follow? No symmetry, that's the secret, no symmetry."

"You've captured the pulse of what's happening," Renata said, "and at a very healthy markup."

"The markup's for my creativity," Raoul said. "They're selling like hotcakes."

The second course came. The plate in front of Alice contained a small lamb chop with a paper ruffle, two string beans, a sprig of parsley, and a radish carved like a rose.

The wine was poured.

Alice looked around the table for bread. There was none. Her lamb was gone with three bites. She carved the last bit off the bone. She ate the string beans one at a time. She ate the radish. She looked around at the others. Everyone else had finished too, in record time, except for Helaine, who hadn't touched anything and was drinking her third glass of wine. Miles was staring glumly at his paper ruffle. Alice waited hopefully, but no one said anything about seconds. She ate the parsley sprig.

"And what is *Elegance Today!* saying about skirt lengths?" Iris asked Helaine.

"Down, down, down! We are all tired of legs, aren't we?" Helaine looked around the table for nods of assent. "We're just putting the September book to bed. The 'Dress for Success' issue. And I say, 'Away with the dreary little gray suit! Welcome the rich colors of fall—Auburn! Persimmon! And why not tuck some fresh autumn leaves in your breast pocket?' " Helaine sighed. "The responsibility! What if all the little shopgirls go out and denude the trees?"

"It is a burden," Renata put in.

Alice watched the conversation bounce among Helaine, Iris, and Renata.

"The Fabric Institute's forecast . . ." Renata was saying.

"In Paris," Helaine said, "it's the year of the *bodice*. . . . Laurent is definitely . . ."

"The Italian knits are so . . ."

"I'm afraid the sun is setting on the British designers. . . ."

"Speaking of the international situation," Iris said, "did anyone happen to see the president's press conference on Latin America?"

"Yeah, man, I saw it," Raoul said.

"Did you notice Barbara Walters's suit? That was *not* an Adolfo!"

Dessert was served. Each plate held a delicately fluted slice of peach and a thin translucent slice of kiwi, surrounded by violets.

Alice watched Iris pick up a small fat fork and she did the same. Iris nodded approval.

Alice looked around. No one ate the violets.

"Brandy in the living room," Iris said. "Girls, if you'd like to walk around the grounds . . . Perhaps Alice would enjoy seeing the garden."

"I wouldn't mind a brandy," Kerstin said.

Iris stared at her coldly.

"Let's take a walk," Kerstin said. "I'll show you the garden."

They drifted out to the patio.

"Do you feel like we've been sent to the children's room?" Jessica said.

"I felt so dumb," Alice said. "I couldn't think of anything to say to them."

"Don't worry," Jessica said. "We're decoration."

"And Miles," Kerstin giggled. "He never talks. Isn't he so handsome, though?"

"I was so afraid my stomach would rumble," Alice said.

Kerstin laughed. "Someone should have warned you to have lunch before Iris's lunch."

"No one can actually live on the Iris Martin diet," Jessica said. "Not even Iris."

"Not even Iris?"

"I hear she gorges on Hershey bars—and does the finger-down-the-throat routine," Jessica said. "I honestly don't think I can sit through another one of her afternoons."

"I'm kind of excited to be here," Alice said, "and she's teaching us all this stuff. She has our best interests at heart. . . ."

"Crap," Jessica said. "This is a business. You get your bookings and she gets her twenty percent. That's it."

"But it's like a family, isn't it?" Alice said. "And Iris Martin is like a mother to all her girls. . . . They even get to live with her sometimes. . . ."

"Like I did?" Kerstin laughed. "It was so funny. Me in one bedroom and Iris in another and poor Miles! He was torn between pay and pleasure and he was so exhausted!"

Alice looked at Kerstin. Was she kidding or what? Kerstin winked.

"Don't get snowed by Iris," Jessica said. "She's not your mother, okay? You'd better be clear on that. She'll cut loose any 'daughter' who doesn't make thirty thousand in billings."

Alice felt a stab of fear.

"Her interests and your interests are not necessarily the same; Iris is looking at her profit margin. It *is* an excellent agency, but you're as good as your last tearsheet and there are no pension plans for models. . . ."

What was she talking about anyway, Alice thought, and who cared about pension plans?

Jessica sighed. "This day is endless. . . . I guess I'd better not leave early, though."

"You'd better not," Kerstin said. "Iris was angry before." Jessica was too serious and Iris even said she had a bad attitude. Kerstin was more like she'd expect a model to be— laughing and sparkling and full of life. And she was so beautiful!

"What happens next?" Alice asked.

"They'll call us for Trivial Pursuit. Then Kenneth drives us back," Kerstin said. "What are you doing after this?"

Alice shrugged. "Just going home, I guess."

"On Saturday night? You can't! It's Saturday night *live* in New York! I'm going dancing with some very interesting men and I know they'd love to meet you. . . ."

"Me?"

"Why don't you have the car drop you at my place? You don't even have to go home first, I'll lend you something to wear." She giggled. "We *have* to wear the same size—we're Iris Martin girls!"

"Would that be okay?"

"Sure! It'll be a fun night!"

It was all happening. John Alveira and then being invited to this beautiful house and now going dancing with someone like Kerstin! It was all starting to happen for her!

15

While Kerstin showered, Alice looked out of the living room window. It was twilight and the lights of the city were twinkling on in the blue-gray haze. Far below, she could see the arc of the 59th Street Bridge shimmering in the East River and the hypnotic movement of headlights. It was electric, beckoning, pulsing with possibilities. It seemed like the whole world was getting ready for something wonderful on Saturday night and here she was, Alice Lonner, in Kerstin's luxury apartment, getting ready, too.

Kerstin's scream from the bedroom shattered the moment. "What happened?" Alice rushed to her. "What's wrong?"

"Look! Oh, God! Look!" Kerstin was inches from the full-length mirror and Alice saw the reflection of her frightened expression.

126

"What—?"

"Look, here. I don't know what to do!" Her white terrycloth bathrobe was pulled past her shoulder to expose a bump. She pointed to it, red against the fragile, milky skin. "I think it's a mosquito bite!"

"Are you allergic or something?" Rosie's cousin Katherine had almost died from a bee bite.

"No, no, but look at it! It's *ugly!* It must have been at Iris's. . . ." Kerstin's eyes never wavered from the mirror.

"Well, if it's only a mosquito bite . . . Do you have calamine or something? If it itches—"

Kerstin let the robe drop at her feet. "Even cover-up won't help. It's a *bump*." She stared at herself, at the pale blonde hair curving over white shoulders, at the firm breasts. Her voice became monotone. "I had pounds of sunblock, but I never thought of insects. I never thought."

Alice shrugged. "Well—" She had been about to say, "so what," but Kerstin wasn't paying attention to her.

"I have to think of something. I have to be perfect. Maybe cover-up . . ." She sighed deeply. "Powder and cover-up. Oh, why doesn't it go away! . . . Go ahead and take your shower, if you want to. I'll think of something." She stared at herself, transfixed. She seemed soothed by her own image.

In the bathroom, Alice pulled off her jeans and shirt. There was a glass-enclosed shower stall, and Alice got into it gratefully and luxuriated in the stream of hot water. It seemed silly for Kerstin to get so upset. What was the big deal with a mosquito bite? She scrubbed hard with perfumed soap. No more baths in the kitchen, she thought. If modeling could get Kerstin all of this . . . Maybe she wouldn't be able to get a place so high up, all new and with a doorman and a fountain in front of the building, it was really great, but she'd get something nice. She looked at her soap-covered body. She wasn't perfect. There was the scar at her knee, but Iris knew about that already, so that was okay. She ran her hands over her skin and, mostly, it felt smooth and slippery. Her elbows were rough. She'd take better care of herself. She'd be careful, the way Iris said, of getting every speck of makeup off her face and rinsing, rinsing, rinsing a million times. . . .

She took a towel from the holder and stepped into it and— it was warm! She felt the towel bar. Wow, it was heated! This was great!

She wrapped herself in the towel and tucked it in to cover up before she went back to the bedroom. She was relieved to see that Kerstin was cheerful again.

"Help yourself," she said, gesturing at the dressing table. "And don't worry, we have loads of time. They won't be here before ten. Nothing starts early." She was applying silver polish to her toes. She was nude and Alice could see she was a natural blonde. She sat on the bed, her foot extended, under the glow of a lamp. There was a translucence about her skin that made her radiant.

An array of makeup on the dressing table—pots, tubes, bottles, brushes—was scattered in confusion. Alice didn't see Damian's exact colors, but there was more than enough to work with. She started to apply ivory foundation.

"You're so beautiful," Alice said shyly. "I didn't think you needed makeup at all."

"I wear it at night," Kerstin said. "I like to look silvery. . . . I don't know, maybe I'll wear a red dress and dark, dark red lips. We'll pick something for you. . . . Oh, this will be fun! There's a party after at Pookie's townhouse—wait till you see it!"

"Pookie?"

"Pookie," Kerstin giggled. "He's Robert Richmond, you know, the tobacco family?"

"Listen, I hope they won't mind . . . I mean, me coming along . . ."

"Oh, no. They *love* models."

"I don't know about Pookie's townhouse," Alice said, "but I think *your* apartment's great."

"Oh, but Pookie's is spectacular! Well, yes, this is okay."

"It's so nice. How long did it take you? Once you started working, how long before you could afford—?"

"The rent?" Kerstin laughed. "I don't exactly pay for it. Oh, I could have taken a little place, a *much* smaller bedroom like a closet and facing a brick wall. I was almost about to sign the lease, and then Max came along just in time. It was so lucky."

"Max?" Alice looked around. There was no sign of anything but Kerstin's things.

"Oh, he doesn't *live* here! I would never have that."

"Then how—?" The mascara brush remained suspended in Alice's hand.

"He's just a sweet old man, like an old teddy bear. He has a family someplace—oh, someplace, I forget the names of suburbs—and he only visits once a week. On Wednesdays. It's no bother, really."

"I don't understand," Alice said. Kerstin looked angelic, ethereal, and she was smiling as though nothing were wrong. But it was wrong, Alice thought, it had to be.

"And very, very rarely on Sunday night, if he can get away. He's no trouble and it makes him very happy. He worked hard all his life and now that he has a lot of money, he's old and, well, it makes him feel proud to have a model waiting here for his visit. It's worth the rent to him and"—Kerstin giggled— "and I'm doing a good deed. I don't do much of anything, nothing kinky, you understand. Mostly, he just likes me to watch him."

"Oh."

"You could find an arrangement. Just make sure it's someone nice who won't be a bother."

"I don't think I—"

"Haven't you ever noticed the limos waiting in front of the agency?"

"I thought they belonged to—I don't know, the top models."

"There are very rich men who like meeting models. It's like wanting to touch a movie star. Being an Iris Martin girl gives you *power*."

"I wouldn't want to—"

"Jessica says they're all perverts." Kerstin shrugged. "Well, I really like this apartment and Max is hardly even in my life. Oh, I'd never, ever be somebody's *mistress*. That's completely different." Kerstin made a face of distaste, wrinkling her delicate nose.

"Didn't you say you had a boyfriend?" Alice asked. "What does he say about all of this?"

"Of course, Kevin. He's at Annapolis and they hardly ever give him time off. He's so sweet and sheltered; he's almost afraid to touch me. It's so sweet. Anyway, Max is only temporary." Kerstin got up and stretched slowly. "How do my toes look? Wait, I never thought—do we wear the same shoe size?"

"Seven," Alice said.

"Oh, dear. Six. I'll find a pair of sandals for you, that should be okay. . . ."

Kerstin rummaged in the overflowing closet and Alice continued, automatically, to apply makeup. Rose blusher on a brush.

Kerstin and her arrangement. It seemed sleazy, but Kerstin made it sound like there was nothing to it. Kerstin looked so wholesome and she was really nice. Maybe Alice was just too dumb about things. Maybe it was different with sophisticated people. Alice lined her lips by rote and felt an edge of discomfort. If a "Max" offered her an apartment, would she take it? There was a dark area she couldn't quite imagine. No, she thought instinctively, she couldn't—but then, maybe nothing was sleazier than a bathtub in the kitchen.

She filled in her lips with Kerstin's red lipstick. Even Claire, she thought, at least *loved* her men. At the beginning, anyway. When Jamie's father first moved in, Claire was all starry-eyed. They couldn't keep their hands off each other and then, at the end, he was yelling and hitting Claire and they were all glad when he finally left. "You can't live with 'em and you can't live without 'em," Claire had said.

More eye shadow. Alice's face in the mirror was beginning to look more like Her. "She" looked like she knew what was going on. The truth was, there was so much Alice didn't know. They had sex education and birth control and all of that in school—but she had nothing to go on. The best she could do was see what felt right, hit or miss. That time with Frank McCall, she had stopped him from going further without quite knowing why. She just didn't trust him enough. It was funny. She used to think Frank McCall was so cool and smooth, but now—well, he was just a kid. He wouldn't even know how to treat her right.

The hangers squealed against the closet bar as Kerstin riffled through them.

"Do you like pastels or black?" Kerstin asked.

"Uh—black, I guess."

"Ooooh, I've got something!" Kerstin held up a black suede miniskirt and matching camisole. "This will be cute on you. See, the front laces up, so it has to fit."

"That's terrific. Thanks! Are you sure—I mean, that looks awfully expensive and I—" Wow, real suede!

"Don't worry. I've got a million clothes." Kerstin tossed it on the bed. "You can return it whenever."

"Thanks, I love it!" She carefully applied her eyelashes.

"Now, what should I wear? I feel like something white. . . ."

Alice worked on her hair. Kerstin didn't have any Tenex, so she couldn't get the top to stand up. Would Kerstin's friends like her? Kerstin said they were in their thirties and that was old. Well, not *that* old. And if she wasn't going to be interested in kids anymore . . . John Alveira was a grown man and she had loved being with him. He made her feel beautiful and he

132

made her laugh and he was someone she could look up to. Maybe Kerstin's friends would be like John Alveira.

Her hair didn't look right and she tried teasing it a little. She felt the nervousness in her stomach. What if she didn't know how to act with them?

"Where are we going?" Alice asked.

"Oh, they'll take us *anywhere* we want. Bailey's or 918 or the Gilded Cave. . . ."

The Gilded Cave! That's where Damian had said everyone went. "I'd like to go to the Gilded Cave!"

"Okay, sure."

This was so exciting—the Gilded Cave and Pookie's townhouse, getting ready in this terrific apartment, and watching Kerstin pulling pretty things out of the overflowing closet. It would be fun, it would be. Just imagine going to all those good places with someone like John Alveira!

Alice put on the suede miniskirt and laced up the camisole. "That's cute on you," Kerstin said. She laughed. "Come on, loosen the laces. You have to let something show. Here, like this. Well, you're kind of small, but even so. . . ."

Her mirror image startled her. The inky black exposing ivory skin to her waist, cropped black hair, smoky eyes, scarlet lips. Kerstin added gold hoop earrings. John should see her now!

She watched Kerstin brush her hair and let it fall long and loose. Kerstin was so lucky—she didn't need any makeup at all, just some silver glitter at her eyes and lip gloss and a bit of mascara. She put on a white satin miniskirt and a white angora tank top edged with pearls. The effect, Alice thought, was breathtaking.

Kerstin frowned into the mirror. "I don't know. Something is off." She brushed a bit of pink blush into the line of her cleavage. "How do I look?" She fastened pearl drops at her ears.

"Very beautiful, Kerstin."

"That mosquito bite! It shows, doesn't it?"

"No, not really. . . ."

"It does! It spoils everything!" She pulled the strap of her sweater over the bump. "It's a defect!"

"Well, now it's covered."

"But I know it's there!" Her voice was high with distress.

Alice looked at their reflections side by side. "Wow, we look like something out of a magazine!"

"Of course," Kerstin said.

Of course, Alice thought, of course we do. That's what this evening would be—straight out of the pages of a glamorous fashion magazine.

16

The Gilded Cave was tucked between decaying factories on West Street. There was a clamoring, pleading throng lined up outside the entrance, barely held back by the velvet rope.

"Bridge and tunnel," Kerstin said, gesturing at them airily.

Alice felt herself being steered by Thornton as she, Kerstin, Thornton, Tommy, and Hans swept past the crowd. The bouncer greeted them effusively as he cleared a path. Hans, Kerstin had told her earlier, was an Austrian prince. She watched him as he put his arm around the bouncer and slipped something into his palm. A genuine prince—Claire and Rosie would love that!

"I don't have any ID," Alice whispered to Kerstin.

"Oh, don't worry. Tommy knows *everybody!*"

Down a flight of stairs and then the impact of the Gilded

Cave hit Alice all at once. First the frantic high-decibel beat of the music. The smell—mingled perfumes, sweat, liquor, and basement dampness. Strobe lights pulsing in reds, violets, and greens. A sea of dancers on the huge floor, moving disjointedly to the contagious rhythm, caught in flashing lights. The room itself was an enormous, dark cave, built on two levels, with offshoots of smaller caves. Gold-plated stone-age implements dangled from walls decorated with bisons in fluorescent paint, stalactites hung from the ceiling, waiters roamed in leopard loincloths, fur throws softened booths on the periphery.

"This way, darlin','" Thornton said, his hand on the bare skin of Alice's shoulder, as they were led to a table. He had been calling her "darlin' " all along, smiling with his mouth, his eyes sliding over her, never really meeting hers. He was a little shorter than she was, solidly built, and his shirt had a monogram. Hans was the one she liked best; he looked younger than the other two and he was the most lively and attractive.

"I will connect with you later at Pookie's, yes?" Hans said. He bent over Kerstin and tilted her face up with both hands. "Ah, *eine Schonheit*, lovely Kerstin," and kissed her on the mouth. Alice was surprised that Tommy, who seemed to be with Kerstin, didn't even blink. "So," Hans said with a wave of his hand, "I will see you," and wended his way through the crowd to the dance floor.

"He seems like fun," Alice said.

"Oh, yes," Kerstin giggled. "He is so funny!"

"He's certifiably crazy," Tommy said. "He likes to strip naked and play the drums."

136

"He did, he really did," Kerstin said, "at the Austrian embassy party. You never know what he will do next."

The waiter came for their orders. Alice hesitated. She waited to hear what Kerstin would have.

"A pink squirrel," Kerstin said.

"Me, too," Alice echoed.

Tommy ordered Black Label and Thornton said, "Mother's milk on the rocks."

"Mother's milk?" Alice asked.

"Beefeater gin, darlin'," he said. He put his arm around her shoulder and Alice tensed.

Tommy and Kerstin had their heads together, whispering, Kerstin laughing.

Alice searched for something to say to Thornton. "What do you do?"

"Import, export," he said.

"Well, like what?"

"A little of this, a little of that." He leaned his head closer to her. "We don't want to talk business, sweetheart."

Conversation was almost impossible, anyway. The band pounded the music, and the dancers were chanting along with the refrain. "Way to go! Hey, hey, way to go!" It was contagious, and Alice's foot tapped in time. This place was really something! She'd remember every detail.

Thornton stroked her neck, and Alice's foot stopped dead. She shivered.

"What's the matter?" he said.

"Nothing." Alice readjusted in her chair.

After the first round, they got up to dance. The drink left

a sticky sweet residue on Alice's tongue. She caught a glimpse of Kerstin in silhouette, gyrating, arms held high. The singer's voice was hoarse and intense. Alice moved self-consciously; she couldn't let go into the throbbing beat. Thornton's face flashed green and lavender in front of her.

At the table, there were more drinks and Alice dutifully sipped hers. Tommy was telling a long story, punctuated by Kerstin's giggle, and Alice strained to hear over the noise. Thornton laughed with them, leaning over the table, and Alice forced a smile.

"Happy, darlin'?" Thornton looked bored.

Alice nodded mutely.

His arm was around her shoulder, and then his finger idly traced the line of her skin between the lacing of her camisole. Right between her breasts! Alice stiffened and moved back, back into the chair. She felt frozen.

"What's wrong with you?" he said angrily.

Alice couldn't meet his eyes. Her teeth were beginning to chatter.

"What is this ingenue act?" He was staring at her coldly. "How old *are* you?"

"Fourteen," she said through numb lips, shamed.

Thornton exploded. "That's great, Kerstin! That's really unbelievable! Set me up with jailbait! Terrific!"

Kerstin slowly turned her head from Tommy. "I'm sorry. I didn't think."

"Damn right you didn't think!" He slammed the table furiously. "We were taking her to Pookie's? What are you, out of your mind?"

"Well, I—" Kerstin started.

"What're you trying to do to me? A Roman Polanski case?"

"I said I was sorry."

Thornton shook his head in disgust and turned to his drink. Tommy stared hard at Alice. "You are one dumb broad," he said to Kerstin.

Alice looked at Kerstin. Kerstin's eyes shifted away. They seemed glazed.

The moment passed. Tommy signaled the waiter for another round. Thornton was watching the dancers, his back to her. Tommy and Kerstin had their heads together, and she heard Kerstin's high giggle. She sat in silence, a pariah, grateful for the dim light. She had to get away. The ladies' room. She could go to the ladies' room.

"Excuse me," she said, forcing her legs to stand. Thornton never looked up at her.

Alice sat down at the long dressing table in the ladies' room and looked at herself in the brightly lit mirror. "She" looked back, beautiful, inky black suede and black hair against white skin and scarlet lips.

There were some women near her, applying lipstick and chattering. "Did you see Madonna come in? Her dress is . . ." "Who was that with her?" In the mirror, Alice could see someone doing a line of coke in the half-open stall behind her. "Who does her hair, do you know?" The stalactites hanging from the ceiling, even here, were obviously plastic in the bright light.

Alice looked in the mirror and "She" looked back until it didn't matter anymore. Thornton was a middle-aged jerk and she'd never have to see him again. It didn't matter. She was beautiful and there'd be other nights and other places. She could live without ever knowing what the deal was at Pookie's. She didn't have to go back. She could leave and return Kerstin's things some other time. And she'd be a *great* model. John Alveira said so. She didn't have to let anyone put her down.

She walked through the swinging door back into the confusion and din.

"Alice Lonner! The divine Alice Lonner!" A familiar voice behind her.

"Damian!" Oh, she was glad to see him!

"So you finally made it to the Cave. What did I tell you, isn't it heaven?" He was bopping along in time to the music. "What *happened* to your eyes? That's not my sienna and gold."

"I had to borrow someone else's stuff and—"

"It's not bad, not bad at all. I would *love* to do an evening look for you. . . ." His hands were in her hair, rearranging, pushing up tufts.

"I didn't have any Tenex with me and—"

"Poor baby. *C'est la vie.* But you look *devastating!*"

He took her hand and led her through the crush. The band had taken a break and now there was a Prince record blaring. He broke ground in front of her, long and lean in a skin-tight red jumpsuit, his hips snaking to the beat. It was infectious and she followed his moves as they worked their way to the dance floor.

This time, the beat pulsed through her body and she danced loose and free. Damian was a terrific dancer and his teeth glinted violet in the light as he laughed. Then there was a smoke effect and she danced her way through billows of gray. This is the way it should be, she thought. Damian was so much fun to be with and the Gilded Cave was wonderful. Then there were Damian's friends, Serge and Lon and Jack and names she couldn't remember, all young and lean and animated. She danced with Lon and the band came on again and she found her way back to Damian.

Kerstin appeared in front of her. "We're leaving, Alice. Will you be okay?"

"Oh, sure," Alice said.

"All right, then. See you."

She watched Kerstin's back as she was swallowed up by the crowd. The band went into its signature song and they all chanted "Way to go! Hey, hey, way to go!" as they moved under the flashing lights. She was so happy to be part of it, right in the middle of things! The smell of sweat and perfume was strong and a tall black man in gold parachute pants was doing break moves, cheered on by the crowd.

"You got any poppers left?" Serge said.

"Here," Damian said, and then to Alice, "You want one?"

Alice hesitated.

"Try it. You'll never know until you try."

Alice would have, because Damian and his friends were so happy and energetic and fun—but the thought of Jamie made her shake her head no. Claire was bad enough. If *she* got messed up on something, what would Jamie do?

The music swirled and swirled around them, and Damian danced with Lon and then with Serge, and she danced with all of them until she was limp.

There was champagne at their table and Damian poured a glass for Alice.

"Isn't she divine?" Damian said. "My creation."

"Mmmm, lovely," Lon said. "Where did you find that outfit? North Beach Leather?"

"I don't know, it's a friend's. . . ." Alice said.

"They have a *marvelous* black leather jumpsuit. You would *love* it, Damian; we should get it for your birthday."

"There'll be a bash on my birthday. You have to come, Alice, it will be fantastic! Invite her, Lon."

"Fine, fine, but I am *not* inviting George Verdun."

"It's *my* birthday and I especially want George there."

Lon looked stricken. "Well, if that's the way you feel. . . ." He rose abruptly and walked away.

Damian looked after him. "God, he's in a snit again! I have to go after him. He's so sensitive."

Serge and Jack and some of the others were at the table, trading private barbed witticisms. Alice sat apart, hoping Damian would come back. The music was wearing down and she noticed the lines of fatigue on Serge's face. They weren't all that young.

What was wrong with her anyway, Alice thought. She should have realized Damian and his friends were gay. She didn't belong. She was a fifth wheel. She sat at the table a little longer, feeling awkward and ignored.

"I have to go," Alice said. "Please tell Damian I couldn't wait for him."

Serge looked up, surprised to see she was still there. "Don't worry about Damian, he's probably *busy* right now. . . ." They all laughed.

142

The pounding drums had been echoing in her head and, at first, Alice enjoyed the quiet of the street outside. It must be close to dawn, she thought, but it was still dark and it was soothing after hours of flashing colors in her eyes. Her legs felt worn-down tired and she walked slowly in the unfamiliar high-heeled sandals.

There was no traffic at all on West Street. Cars sped by on the adjoining West Side Drive; the beams of their headlights did not reach the dark, deserted sidewalk. She passed silent warehouses blending into shadows. She saw the squat Pier 40 terminal across the street and smelled the river. She passed wire fencing and rotting piers and a garage with a fleet of slumbering yellow trucks parked in a row outside. The click of her heels was the only sound.

A shadow moved in a doorway. "Hey, mama!"

Alice caught her breath and walked as fast as the high heels would allow. Where was she—the intersection of West and Morton—there had to be a subway somewhere, east, away from the river. She was all alone and her long bare legs stood out under lamplight.

"What's the rush, pretty mama?" from behind her.

The flicker of fear made her walk faster, wobbling. The cars whizzing by on the Drive would never see or hear her. . . . Don't be a baby, she thought. She was street smart, right? If she were in jeans and sneakers, more like herself, maybe she could handle it. Dressed this way, she felt exposed.

She took off the high heels and ran barefoot through the sidestreets, the miniskirt restricting her stride. A bottle crashed near her, splintering and tinkling. Finally, a subway! More light here, huddled shapes in doorways. Someone on the cor-

ner, gesticulating obscenely at her. The subway entrance—
and the sign: token booth closed, use west entrance. There
was a stitch in her side and where was the west entrance? The
subway would be a horror show at this hour, anyway. Maybe
a cab would come by. If only she had enough money for a
cab— She rummaged through her purse—comb, brush, tissue, lip gloss—and then it hit her. She could clearly see the
crumpled dollar bills left in her jeans pocket at Kerstin's house.

Alice bit her lip. The subway stairs loomed dark and lonely,
smelling of urine. Could she jump the turnstiles—no, they
would be locked. She was caught in a nightmare.

A car cruised by slowly and stopped. "How much do you
get?"

She quickly walked away and the car moved on. She bit
down hard on her lip and tasted blood. She couldn't go back
to the Gilded Cave. Kerstin was long gone and Damian, too.
She forced herself to breathe slowly, to keep down the panic.
She had to think.

John Alveira's was nearby, within walking distance, anyway.
She could go to John Alveira's! She let out a long, shaky breath.
She walked at the edge of the sidewalks, warily checking the
dark doorways. She swallowed down the sick taste rising from
champagne and pink squirrels. She was limping now—something had cut her foot—and fighting back tears.

She felt weak with relief when she arrived on Mercer Street.
Oh, please, John, she thought, please, please be home.

17

John Alveira's block was empty and especially dark; a streetlamp had been vandalized. Alice heard footsteps behind her. She looked over her shoulder; nothing was there, but her pace quickened and all her senses were on alert. A little more to go, she told herself, only a little more.

Finally, she was outside his building. She rang the downstairs bell and waited. She tried the entrance door, turning the knob furiously. It was locked. She rang and rang, slumped against the rough stone of the doorway. She couldn't go another step. She had counted on John Alveira! She sagged with disappointment and rang again, automatically, hopelessly. And then—a prayer answered—she heard a window open above her and then his voice, angry.

"Who is it? What do you want?"

"It's me, Alice," she said. It came out a whisper. She forced her voice to function. "Alice! Alice Lonner!"

"Alice? What the—?"

He buzzed and Alice pushed open the door. She entered the freight elevator and, as it creaked upward, she put on the high-heeled sandals. Her feet were dirty and cut.

He was standing in the doorway of the loft. "Do you know what time it is?" He was in a T-shirt and undershorts, and his hair was tousled. She was aware of the intimacy of seeing him that way.

"I'm sorry," she said. "Did I wake you?"

"Hell, no," he said. "It's only four in the morning." His voice was rough and sarcastic.

She hadn't expected that. She'd expected him to be nice; he'd been so nice and funny when he took her to Ferrara's. She'd been so sure he liked her. Well, she'd messed up everything else tonight. She could have been wrong about him, too.

"I'm sorry I bothered you," she said stiffly. "Look, I'll just go." She took a step back and stopped. She had nowhere to go, there was no place in the world where she belonged.

"Don't be silly, come in." He was rubbing his temples. "You're too sensitive."

"I left . . . my money in . . . my jeans. If you could . . . could lend me cab fare, I'll go." She felt tears waiting just under the surface, putting pressure behind her eyes.

"I don't wake up charming, Alice, but I'm up now and listening. What's going on?"

"I was counting on you and then you sounded so mean and—"

146

"I'll help you if I can, but—" He had his arm around her, comforting. "—but I'm not exactly someone to *count* on. What's going on?"

He was leading her past the studio, into the living area. Only the light near his bed was on, illuminating a small circle. The rest of the loft was in shadows. The faint scent of developing fluid floated in the air.

"Tell me about it," he said.

She curled up tight on his couch, legs tucked beneath her, sandals kicked off. The dark warmth of the loft was comfortable.

"I was at the Gilded Cave. That's where I came from."

"So, you're making the scene."

"Do you go there? I wish I had run into you there!"

"No. I lost my taste for that somewhere between 54 and Limelight."

"You did? Why? I don't think I'd ever—"

"We're listening to your story, Alice, not mine. What happened?"

"I was with Kerstin and her friends and . . . he treated me like—like I wasn't even human. Because of being jailbait." The word brought a flush of humiliation. She was grateful for the darkness shielding her face.

"Kerstin Ronvig?"

"Yes."

He whistled softly. "You cruised right into the fast lane, kitten."

"I felt so—so awkward and stupid! I sat there like a dumb lump! And then I was so glad to see Damian, and it was so much fun, but I was out of place with his crowd, too, and I didn't realize, until I felt like a real jerk. So I left, and a car cruised by and thought I was a *hooker*—and I didn't have any money, I'd left it all at Kerstin's, and I was really scared."

"Sounds like an eventful evening."

She looked up at him. "That wasn't like me. I never get that scared. I could always handle myself."

"The way you're dressed makes you more vulnerable."

"I thought I looked good."

"You do look good, Alice. The problem is, you're not ready to keep up with what you look like." He grinned. "That could be a costume for an S&M ball."

"I know. I don't fit in anywhere. Not anywhere." That's the way she had felt before; she didn't entirely feel it now. She liked the way he had called her "kitten."

"Kerstin's friends aren't the whole world. Maybe she's the one who's off base."

"It wasn't that I didn't *want* to be like Kerstin. I just couldn't."

She rubbed the heel of her foot where it had been cut. There didn't seem to be any glass.

"Kerstin isn't that hard to emulate. You don't really want to, do you, Alice?"

"I guess not," she said. "I don't know where I fit in anymore. I've outgrown the kids at school. I can't go back to—" She spoke slowly, discovering her thoughts as she found the words. "I don't belong with Kerstin or Damian. I don't know where. . . . Except for you. I feel real with you."

The darkness hid his expression, too. "You look exhausted. Do you want me to call a cab? Do you want to get your bearings for a while?"

She couldn't face the street again, or coping with a cab driver. . . . "Could I stay? Could I crash on the couch until morning? I feel like I can't take another step."

"Sure, no problem."

She felt her feet. "Could I take a shower or something?" It wasn't just her feet; she felt grimy all over. "I won't bother you, honest. Go back to sleep. I'll be very quiet."

"It's okay. I'm up," he said.

Suddenly a light was turned on, in her eyes, making her squint. "What?"

"I'm going to take a couple of shots of you. . . ."

"Like this?" She felt the night's makeup caked on her face. She was too tired to even think about posing. "Why?" She had to look terrible.

He already had the camera in his hand.

"I'd better comb my hair," she said wearily.

"No," he said.

She started to tighten the lacing at the front of her camisole. It had loosened as she was running.

"No! Leave it alone!" Click.

"But before you said—" She looked at him, puzzled.

Click. "That's fine." Click. "That's great."

"John—why are you taking all these pictures of me?"

"I guess because I'm fascinated by the way you look. The truth is, I haven't been this interested in photographing anything for a long time."

She felt disheveled and she was confused by the intensity with which he was studying her. She was glad when he released her to take a shower.

She repeated his words over and over to herself as she

scrubbed in the shower. "Fascinated by the way you look."
He did care for her! He thought she was—fascinating. She let
the water pour over her, for the second time in this long, long
day, and she felt warm and bubbly inside. The lost feeling
and fatigue had washed away. "Fascinated."

She dried off—was this his towel, had it touched his body—
and she felt a little shiver at the very bottom of her stomach.
She put on the navy velour robe he had given her. It enveloped
her, much too large, belted tight into voluminous folds. He
was so easy to talk to. And there was something about his
face—lived-in, sometimes sad—that moved her. He'd been
on her mind ever since Ferrara's. If John Alveira touched her,
she wouldn't be a lump.

She came out of the bathroom and he laughed when he
saw her in his robe. She raised her arms, letting the fabric
hang down, and turned around for him. Click. There were
tags attached to the sleeves. She read them: Pierre Cardin.
Large.

"Is this brand-new?" she asked.

"No, I never wear a robe."

"Then why did you—?"

"It was a gift. Last Christmas."

"Oh. Who gave it to you?" She felt a little stab.

"A friend, Alice."

"A good friend?"

"No, only my bad friends give me presents."

"I really hate it when you're sarcastic. . . . What's her
name?"

"Susan."

"Susan. Is she a model?"

"No. Photographers and models are business only. Didn't Iris Martin tell you that?"

"Rules are meant to be broken," Alice said.

"Not that one," he said seriously. "It *is* a business, and that kind of entanglement would mean a lot of problems."

"Well, what does Susan do?"

"Come on, lay off."

"Why can't you tell me? What does she do?"

"She does PR for the Mayor's office."

"Oh. She sounds smart. . . . Does she *fascinate* you?"

He laughed. "No, she doesn't *fascinate* me. Okay, brat, let's call it a night."

He had put a pillow and blanket on the couch for her. Wrapped in the robe and under the blanket, she was rosy and warm. She watched him walk across the width of the loft. Then the light was out and she heard the creak of his bed. She wished he had tucked her in. She wished he had kissed her good night.

"Good night, John," she called across the vast space.

"Sleep tight," he answered. There was a final sound to his voice. The bed creaked again as he turned over.

Her eyes became accustomed to the dark. A buzz came from the massive shape of the refrigerator. The bed across the room was a dark mound; she couldn't distinguish his shape. There was silence. Faint light seeped in through the windows. She smelled stale smoke and ashes. She was wide awake.

"Does anyone ever call you Johnny?" she called.

No answer.

John Alveira. She catalogued the facts about John Alveira. He smoked too much. He never wore a robe. He slept in his underwear. He used Gillette after-shave and Ivory soap. He loved sweets. He had a refrigerator full of beer. He had a quizzical look that put lines in his forehead. He looked tough—until he smiled. He really *listened*, with all his attention, his incredibly blue eyes looking through her. John Alveira.

She couldn't sleep. She thought about the evening at the Gilded Cave. She thought about the fevered bodies, the hoarse chanting, the throbbing beat, the thick hot mood in the air. She didn't want to sleep. There was too much to think about. She thought she heard his faint breaths across the room. She loved John Alveira, and she missed him so much it made her throat ache.

She tiptoed across the room and sat softly on his bed. She watched him sleep, on his back, one arm flung wide. She watched him sleep for a long time. She was filled with tenderness. She thought the words—"love," "tenderness," "passion." She was drawn to him, pulled as to a magnet, and she lowered her body next to his. She brushed her lips softly against his.

He sat straight up, an abrupt move, pulling her up roughly.

"Alice! Cut it out!"

"I was feeling lonely. . . . I wanted to say good night to you. . . ." She liked the soft and seductive way her voice sounded.

"Be a good kid and get back to the couch. We're not playing this game." He reached past her for a cigarette and lit up. He took a deep, slow drag.

152

"Is it because of Susan?" she said. "Is she important to you?"

"No, not really."

There was a silence. Alice watched the lit end of the cigarette move up and down.

"Is it because I'm jailbait? Don't worry about that, honest, I—"

"Don't, Alice," he said. "Don't say anything else." He ground out the cigarette and he put his arms around her, one hand in her hair, her face snuggled against his chest. "You had a bad night, I know. You just want to be held. That's all it is, Alice."

She happily inhaled his smell. She hadn't been hugged in a long time—well, except for Jamie. With Jamie, she was always doing the sheltering. It was good to have someone hold her, comfort her—but he was wrong, that wasn't all it was. . . . She closed her eyes and rubbed her cheek against the soft fabric of his T-shirt.

He stroked her hair. "You're a nice kid, Alice. Sometimes I'm a bastard."

"No, you're not. I know for sure you're not." She laughed confidently into the darkness. "A *real* bastard would never admit it."

He was fascinated by her, but he was worried about her age, she thought. And maybe even the photographer-model rule. He'd need time to see that it didn't matter. She'd be irresistible. She'd be grown-up enough to be patient. And for now, being held by him was a beginning.

18

John Alveira had requested Alice for a shoot for *Vogue.*

"That's terrific—and you don't even have a book yet," Billie had said. "Alveira must have really pushed for you on this one."

John Alveira! She was his inspiration—he'd almost said so. Maybe he wanted to see her as much as she wanted to see him. Alice had tried to say something appropriate, business-like, under Billie's interested look. "I'll finally make some money, right? How much do I get for it?"

"Not that much. Editorial work doesn't pay awfully well, but the important thing is the prestige. It's great exposure and a tearsheet from *Vogue* is dynamite for your book."

They assembled on a deserted stretch of beach, well past the sunbathers who were rushing the season at Jones. Alice was surprised at the number of people; this would be nothing like working alone with John in his studio. Alice felt the familiar knot in her stomach. There was John and a skinny young man, his assistant. There was a makeup woman, a hairdresser, a fashion stylist, an editor, an editorial assistant, and a bearded man whose function she never figured out. And another model, Tanya.

Tanya was black and long-limbed. She had a fine-boned face with slanted eyes, set on an elegant neck and framed by long, silky hair. Black was the wrong description, Alice thought; her smooth skin was the warm color of coffee inundated with cream.

They stood together in the sand as a changing tent was being set up.

"This is the absolute pits," Tanya said to Alice.

Alice looked at her, puzzled.

"Have you ever done furs on a beach in June? No, I guess not—you'll see."

"Why are they doing furs *now?*" Alice asked.

"Because they need lead time for the fall issue. Listen, if you start feeling sick, like you're gonna faint, don't be afraid to speak up. I did furs last August in the middle of Park Avenue—you coulda fried eggs on the street—and one of the girls passed out from heat exhaustion. Drink a lot of water during the breaks."

"Okay, I will. . . . Why would they want furs on a beach?" Everyone was busy and no one had explained anything to Alice.

"We're supposed to be on a desert. Gobi Desert for us

primitive exotics. Chee, you'd think they could spring for location! Who're you with?"

"Iris Martin."

"Yeah, she's good. I'm with Satellite. Hey, look at that, here comes Central Casting. . . ."

Alice followed her gaze. Two men covered with dark blue burnooses were approaching on the sand. And then, led by a trainer, a small camel.

"Chee! Those things *bite!*" Tanya exclaimed.

"Especially you, my love, 'cause you're so sweet," John said. He had come up behind them. "Tanya, I want you *fierce* for this. I want sharp, angular moves."

"You got it, baby." Tanya bared her teeth at him and made a guttural, snarling noise.

John laughed. "Perfect."

He put his arm around Alice and drew her away a little. "Alice, don't think about the entourage. It boils down to you and me, just like in the studio. They're going to arrange the coats and poke at your hair and do everything that needs to be done—don't worry about anything. You're a rare, exotic flower opening up for me, you're a mysterious dream girl in the desert. All you have to do is concentrate on that image. Okay?"

Alice nodded.

"Feel relaxed with the furs—don't be impressed, you can drag them in the sand. They're nothing—you are a *queen*, and jewels, furs are throwaway adornments."

"Okay."

"That's my girl."

Tanya and Alice were called into the changing tent. There was barely room to move without bumping elbows. The fashion stylist, a middle-aged woman with a cigarette permanently dangling from her lips, helped them squeeze into skintight bodysuits—gold for Tanya, silver for Alice. She clipped heavy earrings on Alice's lobes, studied them, squinting, and then removed one. She put an armful of bangles on Tanya.

"Let's go, let's go! I want high noon!" John called.

They rushed out of the tent.

His assistant was raking the sand into geometric patterns.

The makeup woman and the hairdresser went to work. Tanya's hair was arranged in a cloud standing out on all sides. Alice sat on a stool while her face and hair were manipulated. She felt the sun beating down on her head. The bodysuit was clinging to her; she was already beginning to sweat.

"What do you think?" the makeup woman asked.

"No, I want much more," the editor said. "This is *fantasy*."

"Body paint on their faces," John said. "I want Tanya gold and Alice silver."

"I don't know," the makeup woman said. "Remember Annushka?"

"It'll be okay," John said. "It's only on their faces."

The makeup woman shrugged. "Well, okay, if you say so."

"What about Annushka?" Alice whispered to her.

"Somebody—not me—painted her with body paint from head to toe, in rainbow colors, it was a fantastic effect, and—uh—nobody realized that it clogged all her pores, her body couldn't breathe and uh—" She was working on Alice's cheeks. "They got her to the emergency room just in time—

157

but don't worry, that was very thick stuff, and like Alveira says, this is just on your face. You'll be fine."

"Come on! I don't want to lose the shadows!" John, impatient.

"Please—could I see?" Alice said.

A mirror was handed to her. It was very different from Damian's makeup, it was very different from anything! Her skin glistened silver, her eyes were exaggerated and shadowed violet to her temples, her lips were very pale and glittery. A mysterious desert dream girl, Alice thought.

"Come on! Move it!"

A golden lynx coat was draped on Tanya, and a floor-length silver fox on Alice. The camel and the men in burnooses were directed in the background. The makeup woman patted perspiration from Tanya's forehead.

"Okay," John said. "Alice, lie down in the sand, on your side. Good. Somebody, arrange the coat. Head up, Alice, look directly at the camera. That's beautiful. Tanya, crouch next to her. Great. Hold it." Click. "One more time." Click.

Alice felt grains of sand itching in the bodysuit. The heat under the fur was incredible. It was a little better when John had her stand up again.

"Bring the camel in, between the girls. Tanya, I want your back, over-shoulder profile." Someone re-draped the coats. "Alice, face Tanya." Click. The camel moved restlessly. It smelled and Alice kept away from its mouth. The hairdresser adjusted her hair. Click. "Terrific!"

Other coats were brought out: black mink for Alice, sable for Tanya. The furs were unbelievable—Alice had never even been near furs like that—but the heat ruined any pleasure in wearing them. Somebody kept mopping the perspiration. Somebody adjusted the sleeves. John told them to extend their arms and whirl around. Alice was almost panting. Click. She wouldn't complain, no matter what. She was going to be perfect for John Alveira. Between poses, she saw Tanya's face set in a grim, determined line.

One of the burnoosed men was brought forward to kneel at Alice's feet. "Get the boots!" The stylist laced high fur-topped suede boots on Alice. "Alice, put your foot on his shoulder, go on, push him right down, come on, haughty, he's your subject!" Click. "Terrific! That's a killer!" Click. "One more time. Chin up." Click.

Then Tanya with the camel. "Arm around his neck, lips parted. Wonderful, Tanya." And then the camel made an unmistakable noise and left a deposit on the sand.

"Chee!" Tanya exclaimed. "Ain't this animal *house-broken?*"

That broke everyone up—even John laughed. Alice caught his eye and she felt a current between them.

"All right, kiddies, take five."

Alice almost tore off the coat. A pitcher of water was passed around and someone had brought orange sections. Alice gratefully sucked at hers. Her bodysuit was soaked. She sat down on the sand, next to the editorial assistant who looked young and approachable.

"Hi, I'm Alice Lonner," she said.

"Well, obviously, I know that," the girl answered. "Your makeup's a mess. You'll have to be done over."

Alice flared. "Well, obviously, I know that!" She got up and walked over to John and watched him fiddle with the lens of the camera.

"How'm I doing?" she said.

"You're an old pro. I knew you'd be great."

"It's so hot, though."

"I know," he said sympathetically. "Wait till you see the proofs and it'll all be worth it. Honestly, everybody thinks you're doing a terrific job."

"Everybody except what's-her-name—that editorial assistant. She's a snot!"

"Why? Was she rude to you?"

"Yes, and I didn't do anything!"

"It's not you," he said. "Look, here's this girl—she probably graduated from some Ivy League school, and she's working for a pittance in this 'glamour' job. Then you come along, gorgeous and half her age, and you're making more today than she does in a month. So she's got to pull a little weight. So what? The editor said you were a good choice and I'll bet she'll use you again."

"Thanks—you know, for calling me for this."

"My pleasure." He smiled and chucked her under the chin. "Get back to work. Go get fixed up."

Her makeup was repaired and Tanya's hair was braided into a long, thick rope. More coats were brought out—seal, curly lamb, beige mink. The wind machine was set up, and while they worked on the battery pack, she had another drink of water. Then she and Tanya stood side by side while the furs rippled in the wind and sand swirled around them, getting into their eyes. "Goddamn monsoon season," Tanya muttered.

160

Through a haze of heat, she stood and reclined, extended a leg or an arm, smiled and pouted, and let the camera love her. Then it was over.

"Great! It's a wrap!"

She felt as though she'd beeen running up a mountain— exhausted, dry-throated, and exhilarated at reaching the top. John kissed Tanya on the cheek and then kissed Alice exactly the same way, but she was sure he gave her shoulder an extra squeeze.

"Kiddo, you done good," he said.

After that, things started happening fast, too fast for Alice to savor the excitement of one situation before she was catapulted into another. It was like a film reeling itself out in flickering sequences.

Click. A photographer on 36th Street, another on 27th. More test shots. Iris smiling, looking over the proofs, shuffling them with John Alveira's. A portfolio: Alice, wide smile. Alice, profile. Alice in flowered hat. Alice pouting, shoulders bare.

Click. A session for a catalogue. Someone pinning a dress to the floor. Pins at sleeve. Can't move, arms aching. Someone combing her hair. Billie's voice. "Catalogues aren't glamour, they're bread and butter. They pay well—" A voucher turned in to the agency, exchanged for a check.

Focus on the pirouette turn. Try it again. Turn. Turn. A runway. Alice in taffeta, Alice in satin. The beat, beat of the music, hot spotlights, zipped in, zipped out, girls rushing undressed backstage, everyone giddy afterwards, laughing, blowing bubbles at the hairdresser.

Dissolve to conference room, CC&B, ad agency. Men in

business suits, can't get all the names straight. Good possibility, one of them says. Pass her book around.

Fade out on school winding down for the year. Kids talking grades, finals. Alice detached. Grades?—she had another catalogue!

Audio up on Billie's voice. Checking in daily, from pay phones, from home. 555-5355 engraved into memory. Zoom in on Billie's words.

"Alice, hi! I've been trying to reach you all morning! This is a *biggie!*"

"I just got through at that catalogue house and—"

"Well, get yourself over to CC&B—can you make it at three? Remember the address?"

"I'm not sure, I—"

"Got a pencil? Two eighty-five Third, fifteenth-floor conference room. They liked you, Alice! They want to see you again!"

"I forgot, what was that one for?"

"The Mayhem girl. Monthly ads, TV, the whole shebang. They want a new face and they're talking two-year contract!"

"Oh, wow! Okay! Billie, is there anything I should say? Or—?"

"No, just look *wild*. That's what they said, they want a *wild* look. I don't know, flare your nostrils at them." Billie laughed.

"Wow, the Mayhem girl! Billie—what is Mayhem?"

"A brand-new perfume. Lorline is just breaking it. Good luck, doll. You've got a good shot!"

19

When Alice arrived in the reception area on the fifteenth floor of CC&B, it was different from the last time. There was no one else waiting and the receptionist was immediately alert and respectful.

"Oh yes, Miss Lonner." She buzzed the intercom. "Mr. Pages will be right out."

"I don't remember, which one was Mr. Pages?"

"Ken Pages, the account exec on Lorline."

She recognized him from before. This time, he came out to escort her into the conference room, and Alice knew. Billie had said she only had a shot at the Mayhem girl, but from the way they were treating her, Alice knew.

"Mr. Lorman wants to meet you," Ken Pages said.

"Who's Mr. Lorman?"

"The *client!*" He seemed somewhat jittery. "CEO for Lorline. He started the company."

Alice was walking in a dream, unnaturally calm, almost sleepy. She *knew.*

Just before he opened the door of the conference room, he said, "Lorman will ask you questions, and just, you know, answer them. Don't be nervous." Alice looked at him. She wasn't the nervous one. It was too unreal. "Okay, here goes."

There was a long rectangular table in the room. Most of the men sitting on both sides looked familiar from the last time. Last week, when she was just part of the crowd of other models. She remembered the art director. This time, they half-stood until she was seated at one end. All except for the man at the other end. He remained seated, amply filling his tilted-back chair. This was Mr. Lorman. He acknowledged the introduction with a nod and a grunt. He was the only one who seemed entirely relaxed—jacket open, silk-shirted stomach bulging out.

"We've seen your book," the art director said. "Very nice. Mr. Lorman would like to look through it."

Alice handed over her portfolio and it was passed the length of the table to Mr. Lorman. He opened it, glanced at a photograph, looked up, and stared at her.

"The shot in the fur coat, sir. It seems to fit the mood we were discussing." Ken Pages rose and started to point it out to him. Mr. Lorman waved him away and Ken Pages sat down.

"How long have you been modeling?" Mr. Lorman said.

"My first real job was for *Vogue* in June. The tearsheet's in there. . . . I signed with the agency in—I guess it was the end of March." Had it really been such a short time ago?

164

"And before that?"

"Before what?"

"Mr. Lorman wants to know what you did before you started modeling," Ken Pages said.

"What, does she need an interpreter?" Mr. Lorman said.

"Oh. I was in school."

"Was it a good school?"

"It was okay."

"My stepdaughter goes to a good school. It'd better be a good school—the bills are pretty damn good!" He snorted a laugh.

The others chuckled politely. Alice stared at him, mystified.

He thumbed through the photographs perfunctorily. The room was silent except for the shuffling of the pages. And then Mr. Lorman put his pinky way up into his nostril.

Alice looked at the others. No one met her eyes; they were all pretending it didn't happen. Mr. Lorman did it again, with his ring finger.

She couldn't believe it. Once Jamie picked his nose in public and Claire slapped his hand and made him cry. And here, this man. . . !

He looked up and caught her astonishment. He shrugged and continued examining the portfolio. Then he put the book down and leaned back comfortably.

"All right, sell yourself."

There was a pause while Alice considered what she had to sell.

"She's a new face," the art director put in, "and even if she's a little inexperienced—"

"Let her talk," Mr. Lorman said. "Are you nervous?"

"No," Alice said. She truly wasn't; he was too bizarre to be intimidating. "It's just that I hadn't thought about it before. . . . My selling point is my face." She turned to show him her profile and then slowly turned back to him. "Photographers tell me I have no bad angles."

"Is that it?" Mr. Lorman said.

"That's it. That's what I do—have a great face."

"Oh, so you think you have a great face, do you?"

"If I don't, then the people who're paying me for it are crazy."

"Well, young lady, Mayhem is the crown jewel of the Lorline line. I've had those Ph.D. chemists working night and day—" Another snorted laugh. "—night and day mixing up the right fragrance. It's gonna be bigger than Chanel No. 5. You think you're good enough to be the Mayhem girl?"

"I don't know exactly the look you want. I'm very versatile; you can see that from my portfolio."

"What kind of lipstick is that?"

"Margeaux." She felt the shock tremors in the room. She hadn't thought . . . well, she didn't have to depend on him like all these other guys.

"That's garbage! What color?"

"Terra Cotta."

"Terrible name. Why aren't you wearing Lorline?"

"I didn't choose it. My makeup man gave it to me." She sounded too apologetic to herself. What was she apologizing for, anyway?

"You should wear Lorline. I'll send you a case. Show it to your makeup man."

"Thanks. I'll do that." Was he really going to send her a *case* of lipstick? This conversation was leaving her numb.

When he was sure Mr. Lorman was finished, the commercial producer spoke up. "The print ads will read 'Wherever she goes, there's . . . Mayhem!' The TV spots will back it up with 'Wherever I am, it's . . . Mayhem!' Of course, it could be a voice-over if absolutely necessary. . . ."

"The Mayhem girl oughta know how to talk," Lorman said. "Have her say it."

"Would you mind saying that line?" the producer said.

"Wherever I am, it's Mayhem?"

"Try it with a beat between 'it's' and the product."

"Wherever I am, it's . . . Mayhem."

"Could you try it again—a longer pause, feature the name. And if you could think of the meaning—give us a devilish gleam in your eyes on 'Mayhem'."

A devilish gleam? Maybe she could widen her eyes and smile a little. "Wherever I am, it's . . . Mayhem!"

"Good. A little more pizzazz?"

"Wherever I am, it's . . . MAYHEM!"

"Okay. Thanks."

No one had anything else to add.

"We'll be in touch," Ken Pages said. "We'd like to hold on to your book."

Alice hesitated.

"Overnight. We'll messenger it back to your agent."

"Oh, okay."

They thanked her for coming in. She felt Mr. Lorman watching her shrewdly as she walked out. She knew they were going to talk about her now and pass around the portfolio and decide about pros and cons—but she had a feeling, she *knew* she was the one. TV spots? Had all of this happened? She went to the elevator like a sleepwalker.

Billie's call came a few days later. "You did it! Iris is ecstatic!"

"The Mayhem girl?"

"That's you! Iris is working out the contract. . . . She wants you in her office on Thursday."

"I'll be there. Thanks, Billie."

"Well, congratulations. All right, doll. 'Bye."

Alice could tell that Billie was disappointed in her lack of excitement. She couldn't react yet. She needed more time to absorb what this might mean for her.

She found the word in Claire's pocket dictionary.

may·hem *n*. **1.** *Law* the offense of maiming a person maliciously **2.** any deliberate destruction

Probably the second definition was more appropriate—but that didn't make too much sense either. Pretty weird for a perfume.

She looked in the mirror and said, "Wherever I am, it's . . . MAYHEM!"

"We got the best deal we possibly could. There were some sticky points, but—" Iris handed Alice a copy of the contract and skimmed through the pages of her copy as she talked. "I'll run through the main points. . . . Paragraph one. Two-year contract to begin July fifteenth, renewal option for an additional one-year term at the same rate. I tried to get an escalation, but they wouldn't budge."

Alice tried hard to concentrate.

"Paragraph two. Guarantees four full-day shoots for print ads per month. Anything additional, more session time, means extra compensation. Paragraph five. TV spots. . . . residuals after every thirteen weeks. . . . You'll have to join the actors' union, you know. . . ."

Alice listened, trying to take it all in.

"Let's see. Paragraph nine is important. You can't model for any Lorline competitor. That means no other makeup, hairspray, soap, lotion, etcetera. That's standard. By the way, they'll use you for more than perfume. 'The Mayhem girl wears Lorline lipstick'—that kind of thing. And there are other restrictions; they don't want you overexposed. Of course, they're paying for that exclusivity. . . . Paragraph 16A— moral turpitude clause. That means this contract is void if your behavior or actions reflect negatively on Lorline."

"Moral turpitude?" Alice echoed.

"No one cares who you sleep with in your personal life but no *Penthouse* centerfolds, no blue movies, no public scandal of any kind. . . . Alice, if you've ever been involved in any sort of porn, *right now* is the time to tell me. Have you?" Iris looked at her severely.

"No!" How could Iris possibly think that!

"All right. Good. Last paragraph covers the agency commission; we deduct it from your payments and then give you a check for the remainder. Well, that's basically it. And then the signatures. You sign, your mother signs . . ."

169

"My mother? What's she got to do with it?"

"You're a minor and she's your legal guardian. You sign, they sign, and then you get a copy to keep. Any questions?"

Questions? Alice was dizzy with rehearsals, escalations, compensation. "No—uh—just, how much do I actually get?"

"Oh, that's spelled out in Paragraph One. Basic annual fee is two hundred thousand, to be paid in bimonthly installments, but you have to remember—"

"Two hundred thousand!"

". . . remember that you can still do fashion work, so—"

Two hundred thousand!

"So you could be earning close to twice that. Before taxes, of course; you should consider a business manager—"

Two hundred thousand! The excitement that had been bottled up was starting to explode. "Dollars? A year?"

"Annually means per year, dear."

Iris went on saying things, lips moving, smiling. They were rich! There had been some money from the jobs she'd done; she'd paid Iris everything she owed, and she'd even bought herself some clothes, and she had the money to get Jamie's bicycle, whenever she had time—but two hundred thousand! She could buy anything! She could do anything! She couldn't sit still.

She left the agency with firecrackers inside. Oh, man! Wow! It had started to rain and she didn't even feel it. She was honest-to-God rich! So what if her new dress got wet? She could toss it out and buy another!

A limousine was hanging around outside the agency, and the man inside called to her. "Need a ride, beautiful?"

"No!" And hadn't Iris said she'd be earning even more? Wow, this was Alice in Wonderland for sure!

"Hey, beautiful! It's raining! Don't you want a nice dry ride?"

"No way! You want to know something, mister? I can buy my own limo any time I want!"

20

"The first thing we're gonna do is get out of this dump," Alice said.

Claire looked overwhelmed. "We really can, can't we?"

"Are we moving?" Jamie was wide-eyed.

Alice's glance swept the cluttered living room with Claire's unmade couch-bed in the center. It had never looked shabbier. "Damn right we are!"

"Where are we moving to?" Jamie asked.

"I don't know. I want a view like Kerstin's and a doorman and a—"

"Will I stay at my school?" Jamie looked scared.

"I guess so, we'll stay in the neighborhood. . . . Hey, wait a minute! You can go to one of those *private* schools!"

"I don't want to! I don't know anybody there!"

"Well, we'll see. The first thing is we get out of here."

"My bicycle was gonna be the first thing. You said, Alice."

"Okay, okay. Soon as I have time to take you shopping."

"When?" he said in a small voice.

"Soon." She turned to Claire. "I want you to start looking right away."

"Gosh," Claire said. "I don't know where. . . ."

"There's plenty of apartments in those luxury high-rises. They're in the paper all the time."

"Luxury high-rises? They rent for two thousand, three thousand." Claire was looking scared, too. "And they'll want first month's rent and last month's and a security deposit and I don't know what-all."

"I'm not *waiting* for anything anymore! Iris can vouch for me. And anyway, I'm doing the first Mayhem shoot next week." Alice brushed away that niggling little feeling of fear. That contract was for sure—wasn't it?

"I can't believe it. It's like I won the lottery!" Claire said. "I was always thinking of all the things I would do if my numbers came up. And they have, haven't they?" She laughed. "And now I can hardly think of anything! I'll tell Office Temporaries to quit calling me and then I'll—"

"Wait a minute," Alice said. "You better wait until I get the first check."

"We'll get a *big* apartment." Claire was getting into the spirit of it. "Three bedrooms and we could get a car and—"

"A car!" Jamie shouted.

"I can't get a driver's license yet," Alice said.

"*I'll* drive. We can go to the beach all summer and—"

She should have known Claire would get carried away, Alice thought. This whole thing was going to be her responsibility. "Maybe—maybe we'd better start off with two bedrooms," she said cautiously, "just until we see how it goes. . . ."

"All right, two. One for you and Jamie and one for me, and we'll get one of those cute—"

"No," Alice said. "I get my own bedroom. You and Jamie can share."

"What?"

"*I* get the master bedroom."

Claire looked surprised.

"And if you're not going to be working, I want you to keep the place *neat*."

A pause and then Claire's enthusiasm bubbled up again. "Alice, you know what? We can get a maid!"

"This isn't the lottery," Alice said. "This isn't a bottomless pit."

Jamie stared, confused, from one to the other.

The photographer for the Mayhem shoot was Terry Gordon. He didn't remember her, of course, from that long-ago day when she waited in his reception room in the fur district. It wasn't like working with John Alveira, but he was nice; he said she was flawless.

It was a long session. The dress they put her in was something else—floor-length clingy red sequins cut down to her navel! There were lots of different poses, all revolving around five men in tuxedos lying down on the floor around her, like they were dead or something. One time, they had her stand with each of her high-heeled feet on a different man's chest. It was hard to keep her balance and she hoped the spike heels weren't killing them. She couldn't figure out what it had to do with perfume.

She talked to one of the tuxedoed guys during a break. His name was Bob McConnell.

"I hope I didn't hurt you before," she said.

"That's okay. I've had to do crazier things."

"Have you been modeling long?" she asked. "Who're you with?"

"For a while, but I'm not a *model*. It's like an extra thing I do; it helps make the payments on the house."

"Oh?"

"We've got a place in Hastings; it's not a bad commute and it's great for the children. . . . In real life, I'm a teacher. Junior high. I have a passion for history. . . ." He smiled wryly. "God, I hope no one spots me in this ad. My face won't show much, I don't think."

"I can't wait for it to come out," Alice said. "I want everybody to see me!"

"It's different for you."

"How do you mean, different?"

"It's different for a girl. I feel kind of sheepish, I guess."

"You sound ashamed of being a model."

"Oh, it's okay. It's legal, right?"

"I don't get it," Alice said. "Why is it different for me?"

"A man's supposed to be more than a pretty face. . . . The funny thing is, I make a hell of a lot more here than with my eighth-graders. . . ."

Alice thought about it for a while. Why was being photogenic absolutely terrific for a girl and not enough for a man?

The next job was the taping for a Mayhem TV commercial. Alice recognized some familiar CC&B faces among the bunch of people in the control room.

They dressed her in emerald green satin, and the hairdresser curved a long green feather around her head. Her costume was wildly out of place among the guys in jeans pushing cables and adjusting wires in the brightly lit studio. Behind her was a set composed of abstract neon signs.

First there was a no-fax rehearsal—a walk-through without camera or facilities. All she had to do was walk straight toward the camera, stop at a mark on the studio floor, and say, "Wherever I am, it's Mayhem." It seemed simple at first, but then she had to say the line over and over again to get it the way they wanted. And they worked on her walk; it had to be fast and exciting.

"All right, let's do it. Take one."

The stage manager signaled her to start and she saw the red light on the camera go on. There were flashing lights all around her. She knew she was doing the walk right and she gave the camera her sexy look and said the line.

The director's voice came over the PA. "Alice, you overstepped the mark. Take two."

She tried not to be distracted by the cameraman and all the other people. She stopped right at the mark and said the line.

"Alice, you can't look down! One more time. Take three."

176

She concentrated on the camera lens and caught just a glimpse of the mark from the corner of her eye.

"That's better," the voice echoed. "More of a rush, you're going somewhere! Take four."

She felt the skirt swirl around her. "Wherever I am, it's . . . MAYHEM!"

"Get rid of that boom shadow!"

The boom operator raised the mike.

"Check the sound level again. And Alice, more punch on Mayhem."

"Wherever I am, it's . . . MAYHEM!"

"Good. Take five."

Her feather loosened and they had to stop and fix it.

There was a buzz in the studio. "Lorman just came in."

Take six. There wasn't enough of a pause between 'it's' and 'Mayhem'.

Take seven. "Wherever I am, it's . . . **MAYHEM!**"

"Perfect! That does it, Alice. You want to come up and see it?"

She went up the stairs to the control room. Mr. Lorman nodded in her direction. Everyone was watching the replay on the monitor. She felt self-conscious—her voice sounded strange, her emphasis on "Mayhem!" with widening eyes, seemed too much. At the same time, she was detached, critically observing Her in green satin and feathers.

"That works," the director said. The CC&B people nodded.

"It's not exciting," Lorman said.

"It will be. We're overdubbing the music and at the end there'll be sirens and fire alarms and—"

"What's that lipstick?" Lorman said. "It's too orange."

The makeup man was called up to the control room. "Lorline's Red Flash, sir."

"It doesn't look right." Lorman frowned. "Fix it."

There were barely audible sighs.

Back to the studio floor. The makeup man rubbed the lipstick off Alice's lips and applied another color. The earphoned stage manager transmitted Lorman's control room pronouncements. Lights were re-set.

Take eight. "Wherever I am, it's . . . **MAYHEM!**" Lorman thought it was too pink. Take nine. Not bright enough.

They decided to solve the lipstick dilemma off-camera. Alice's lips felt rubbed raw as the makeup man went through his arsenal. The crew shifted restlessly as Alice's lips were checked under the lights. "Too harsh," Lorman said. Then, "Very pale." And, "Those lights are washing out the color. Try something else."

The makeup man re-applied lipstick and muttered under his breath, "We're back to Red Flash."

"That's it," Lorman said triumphantly. "That's the one!"

Take ten. Take eleven. Take twelve. Take thirteen. The syllables lost all sense as Alice parroted the line again and again. Her walk had lost its fast, breezy bounce.

Finally, Lorman became bored and left the studio to a chorus of "yes, sir"s.

Hours had gone by and Alice felt drained.

The director's voice came over the PA. "We're going with Take seven. Good job, Alice. Thanks, everybody."

It was all insane, she thought—but then, she could handle a lot of insanity for that kind of money!

The Mayhem money was to be paid in equal bimonthly installments. Alice received the first check from Iris. She took it out of the envelope and looked at it outside the agency door. There it was, in red printed letters. "Pay to the order of Alice Lonner the amount of six thousand six hundred and sixty-six dollars and sixty-seven cents." Was that right? Two hundred thousand minus Iris's twenty percent divided by twenty-four—she needed pencil and paper for this. She'd do it later; anyway, it had to be right and—almost seven thousand dollars!

She went to the bank on Second Avenue where Iris said her check would be accepted. She got on line and waited as it slowly inched toward the teller's window. She shifted from leg to leg. This was the test, she thought. Now she'd find out for sure if she'd been caught up in one of Claire's fantasies.

At the teller's window, she had to sign her name and show the identification card Iris had given her. The teller looked at it closely. Something could still go wrong—but no, she said pleasantly, "How would you like this, Miss Lonner?"

"How?"

"A teller's check or a—"

"Cash! I want it in cash!"

The teller paused. "That'll be just a minute, please. The manager has to get it from the vault. Did you want large bills?"

"Uh—hundreds and twenties," Alice said.

She stepped aside to wait while the teller helped the next person on line. And then, the teller was counting it out, a thick green wad, and it was handed to Alice, and Alice counted, losing track once, having to start all over, and then it was hers! Hundreds and twenties, stuffed in her purse, making lumps in her jeans pockets. She felt the crinkly paper with her fingers. It was hers! It was real! She could do anything— *any*thing she wanted! And there'd always be more. . . .

Stuffed animals and gold chains, dinner for all of them in a *good* restaurant, a new apartment, diamond-stud earrings, a bike for Jamie, paints in all the colors she wanted, a fur like she'd worn for the V*ogue* shoot, quarters for video games— hell, she could buy her own video game!—all danced in Alice's head.

"Have a good day," the teller said.

"Oh, I will!" Alice beamed. "I'll have a great day!"

Outside the bank, people rushed by her in all directions. She wanted to tell someone. Hey mister, she thought, as a man in a business suit passed by, hey mister, I've got seven grand in my pocket! She sailed over the sidewalk.

At 58th Street, she saw the bag lady in her regular spot. This time, she didn't hurry past. The bag lady had a cat on a thin red leash.

"You have a *cat?*" Alice said. She'd never noticed before.

"Oh, me and my Bessie, we've been together a long, long time. Ain't she sweet?"

"She's pretty," Alice said. It was a tabby with smooth, silky fur.

"They won't let animals in those shelters. Those shelters, they're no good. Rob you blind, that's what they do."

The bag lady wasn't scary at all. She was just a person down on her luck.

"Here," Alice said. She pulled a twenty from her pocket. "Get her some cat food."

"That's a whole lot of cat food!" The bag lady chuckled. "Bless you, girlie, bless all your days."

She could be a blessed Lady Bountiful, Alice thought, as she continued her whirl down the street. She could do good deeds—and first, she'd do good deeds for herself! She'd earned it. She ought to celebrate with someone. She ought to do something terrific—John Alveira would make it fun! She could call him—no, she'd just hail a cab and be there in minutes.

"So, what's the emergency this time?" John said as he let her into the loft.

"No emergency—just a lot to tell you," Alice bubbled.

"I'm on a deadline. . . . All right, talk to me while I work."

She talked as she followed him into the darkroom. She could barely make out his expression in the dim glow of the safety light.

". . . and I did the print ad and the TV spot, and Terry Gordon said I was *flawless*, and the CC&B people said—" She hoped she didn't sound too excited, too immature.

He was putting paper into a developing tray. She watched an image of a figure appear and darken. It went into another tray. He lifted the photograph out of the liquid and hung it up to dry. "Sounds like everything's going great."

He was probably used to models with big contracts. But she was too happy to make her tone matter-of-fact. "And today I cashed the first check and it's right here in my pockets!"

He lowered another sheet of paper into the liquid. "What? In cash?"

"Almost seven grand."

He looked up at her. "That's not too bright, Alice." He laughed. She loved the way he laughed. "In your *pockets?*"

"I know. But it makes it *real.*"

"You'd better find out about a business manager and—"

"Now you sound like Iris and Billie."

"They're right, you know. You ought to invest in—"

"I'll do all that later. There'll be more, lots more. I'm going to *spend* this!"

Another photograph was hung up to dry. "What happens next? Do you go on a big shopping spree?"

"I guess. I haven't had time to do anything yet. I promised my little brother a bike and then— That's what I'll do. I'll go on a shopping spree! At Bloomingdale's!"

"You know, that's something I'd like to watch—you running wild at Bloomie's. Okay if I come along?"

"Oh, sure!" He wanted to be with her, and this wasn't professional either. "I have a free day tomorrow—if you have time. . . ."

"I'll make time. You're on, tomorrow."

He was breaking his photographer-model rule for her. He couldn't resist!

"Alice, when we go tomorrow, do me a small favor, okay?"

"Sure, what?"

"Skip the makeup and wear . . . you know, jeans and . . ."

"Jeans? Like these?"

"No, not designer jeans. Don't you have a pair of old—"

"But why?" she wailed. Those old jeans she used to wear? She wanted to dress up for him! "They're torn and—"

"Go along with my idiosyncrasy, okay? Anyway, torn jeans are back in style. . . . Don't look like a model."

"You want me to look like a *kid?*"

He grinned. "Why not? And have your little brother wear something old and scrungy and—"

"You want to take my *brother* along?"

"Come on, Alice, let's not leave him out. How old is he again?"

"Seven."

"Great! We'll have a good time."

"But I don't want—"

"I'd like to meet him. Tomorrow, Lex Avenue entrance of Bloomingdale's at . . . eleven?"

"I thought you'd celebrate with me," Alice said. "Let's go out for champagne! I'm buying!"

"Alice, I'm swamped with work and—"

"Oh, come on, celebrate with me. . . ."

"—and I've got a shoot tonight."

"At night?"

"We're using the Lincoln Center fountain. Evening clothes."

"Oh."

"Go on along, kitten, and I'll see you tomorrow. And hey— I said you'd be a great model, didn't I?"

Alice rode down in the elevator thoughtfully. Maybe he was tired of models and he liked the way she was underneath. But she wasn't that kid in old jeans anymore! Why would he take

Jamie along? That could be a sign that he wanted to know all about her, even her family. And he was going to spend the whole day with her! Suddenly, she had everything she wanted. Things that just a few short months ago she hadn't even known enough to want!

She felt like turning cartwheels in the street. Instead, she hailed a cab, and when they reached her building, she loftily told the driver to keep the change.

21

Alice woke up on Thursday morning, gladly, not dragged out of sleep as usual, not rushed. Jamie was still fast asleep, breathing deeply. She stretched luxuriously in bed, enjoying the anticipation of a whole wonderful day with John Alveira.

The persistent ringing of the telephone in the next room interrupted her mellow feeling. Finally it stopped.

"Alice!" Claire called, hoarse-voiced.

Oh, please, she thought, don't let it be Billie. She tucked her head under the covers. Please, don't let Billie have something for me today, not today of all days!

"Alice, it's for you!"

"Okay, okay, I'll be right there."

She pulled down her T-shirt as she went into the living room. Claire stretched and wandered sleepily into the bathroom.

"Hello?"

"Hi, Alice. It's Rosie."

"Oh, hi!" She had missed Rosie! They hadn't even talked since school was out.

"If you're busy or something . . . I just thought I'd say hello."

"I meant to call you a million times. There's so much to tell you!"

"Yeah, well, I guess . . . So, how is everything?"

"Great." Alice glanced toward the closed bathroom door. She heard Claire running the water. "Rosie, guess what? I met the nicest man." She lowered her voice. "Honestly, I think I'm in love. I'm meeting him today and I'm so excited and—" She'd missed having a girlfriend to talk to! "His name is John Alveira."

"Is he your boyfriend?" Rosie giggled.

"Well, it's kind of different . . . he's older, and—"

"Are you going out with a *college* boy?"

"Uh—no, he's a little older than that."

"Older than college?"

"He's not *old*, he's very handsome and . . . You'd have to see him."

"I don't know, Alice, that sounds kind of . . . I'd think *college* age is too old for us."

"You'd have to meet him, I guess," Alice said. She didn't know how to make Rosie understand. She couldn't even imagine Rosie with John Alveira. "He's a pretty famous photographer."

"It's sure been a long time," Rosie said. "You're with all new people, I guess."

186

"I guess, at work," Alice said. There was a long pause. "How's Mike?"

"Fine. Same as always. . . . So . . ."

"What've you been doing?"

"Not too much. Working on my tan. . . . I might get a part-time job at Burger King."

"Oh. That sounds good."

"What's good? It's minimum wage, Alice, and it's a hassle."

"Oh, right."

"That's something I wanted to ask you about. When we saw your picture in the *Times*—"

"My picture?"

"In this morning's paper."

"*The New York Times?* Me?"

"Didn't you know? In the business section. My dad saw it. There's an announcement about an advertising agency and — Anyway, my dad read it and he said if I wanted to do something like that, he said okay."

"Wow! I haven't even seen it! *The New York Times!*"

"I kind of went to this other agency a while ago, Gotham Models, just to see. They had an ad, models wanted, and I was sort of curious, so . . . They said they'd take me, but I'd have to have pictures for a portfolio and it would cost five hundred dollars and—"

"Rosie, that sounds phony. The legit agencies don't charge you for photos. That sounds like a rip-off."

"That's what my dad thought. Anyway, he wasn't about to go for five hundred. But then we saw your picture in the paper this morning and he said it was the real McCoy. So we were thinking, if you could set up an appointment for me with your agent . . . ?"

"With Iris Martin?"

"The article said you had a six-figure contract, and that sure would beat Burger King, and my dad said it was okay with him. I feel kind of funny asking, but my dad said I ought to, we're best friends and all. . . ."

"Rosie," Alice said slowly. "You have to be a certain height and . . . weight."

"I know. I could lose a few pounds."

"The height, though, and—"

"They could use just my face. I've got a perfect nose, you know that yourself, Alice, and I have awfully good teeth. I could do toothpaste and stuff like that."

"Iris Martin doesn't use models just for faces. There's fashion work and—"

"I don't see why I couldn't . . . I mean, we were always about equal . . . Well, my dad thinks I'm absolutely gorgeous, you know." Rosie's laugh sounded forced. "But aside from him, Mike doesn't think we're that different. He said if *you* could do it . . . He's kind of biased, I guess."

"They look for certain bone structure. . . ."

"Could you set something up for me, Alice, just to see?"

"I—I don't think I really could." There was an uncomfortable silence. "I don't think it would work out."

"I thought there'd be nothing to lose if . . . well . . . I shouldn't have bothered you. I guess I was trying to get out of making hamburgers all summer. . . ." That self-deprecating laugh again. "If you don't think I could . . ."

"It's just that . . ." Alice heard the refrigerator humming in the kitchen. "I know what they look for. Honestly, I do. . . ." Her voice tapered off.

Another silence.

"Look, forget it, Alice. Please forget about it."

Alice swallowed. "Rosie, I'm sorry, I—"

"No problem." She sounded embarrassed.

"Rosie? Maybe we can get together soon. I'd really like to talk."

"I always think you're so busy. How about tomorrow?"

"I'm working tomorrow, I don't know when I'll get through. . . . I get free days; I never know too far in advance. And I have weekends. Is Sunday good?"

"It's my cousin Irene's wedding. I told you about her and her boyfriend and all the problems they were having."

"Mmm-hmm." Alice didn't remember.

Rosie hesitated for a moment. "Well, anyway, they got everything straightened out. I guess I didn't tell you."

"You could sleep over, when I get my new apartment. I'm moving soon."

"Great. It sounds like everything is going great. Listen, Alice, I gotta run now. My mom is waiting for me and—"

"Rosie?"

"So long, Alice. I'll call you. We'll get together real soon, okay?"

Alice put the receiver down slowly. She was all alone in the morning quiet of the apartment with only the refrigerator's sad hum for company. She needed someone, she needed . . . Wait, what had Rosie said. Her picture in *The New York Times*!

She pulled on her jeans and rushed downstairs to the newsstand at First Avenue and bought a copy. She riffled through it frantically, leaning against the kiosk. Business section. There it was, on the third page. Her face in the paper. She felt tingles down her back.

CC&B's new campaign for Lorline will feature model Alice Lonner, recently signed to a six-figure, two-year contract. . . . Lorline's introduction of Mayhem perfume . . . Ken Pages at the helm . . . The account, transferred from . . .

There was nothing else about her, but—wow!—her picture at the top of the column. Someone brushed by her and picked up the *Times*. Her picture was in all those copies on the newsstand. All over the city, the world, even! She felt the heat rising in her face.

She had known the ads and the TV commercial would come out soon, but this was the very first time: Alice Lonner in print in public. She clutched the newspaper. Her arms and legs were charged with electricity. She watched, mesmerized, as people passed by and picked up their copies. They would be reading about *her*. Seeing *her*. She was *somebody*—somebody to write about in newspapers!

"I don't wanna wear those crummy old jeans!"

"You have to!" Alice was wearing her old jeans and T-shirt, the way John had asked her to, so why couldn't Jamie just listen!

"I won't! I'm wearing my new ones!"

"Hurry up and put on the old ones."

"Why?" Jamie demanded. Why did John want them in old clothes, anyway? Maybe he thought they'd have more fun and be more relaxed that way. It didn't make too much sense, but he'd made such a point of it and she didn't want to spoil anything. She had put on just a *little* dab of mascara and blusher.

"Never mind why. Just do it!" Alice bristled with impatience.

"I won't!"

"Then you can't come with us. I'll leave you home."

She saw Jamie's face set in a stubborn line. He wasn't going to give in for anything. He was pale and his mouth was puffed out, holding back tears. He was getting older; he wouldn't cry, no matter what. She softened. What did he have to wear those old jeans for, anyway? And he looked really cute in the new green-and-yellow-striped Izod.

"Okay, okay, never mind, let's go."

She rushed him along 59th Street. He skipped to keep up with her.

"A ten-speed blue Schwinn!" he said. "Remember, a tenspeed."

"I know." He'd only told her a thousand times.

"Why can't we get the bike first?"

"We're going to Bloomingdale's first. They don't have bikes."

"But why can't we get the bike first?"

"I told you! Because we can't drag it all over Bloomingdale's. We'll go to the bike store last."

"I don't wanna go to Bloomingdale's!"

"Cut it out, Jamie. It'll be fun!"

"I don't wanna look at dresses all day."

"We'll look at the other stuff, too. Maybe we'll get things for the new apartment."

"When are we getting the new apartment?"

"Soon. As soon as Ma finds one." She sidestepped past people crowding Lexington Avenue.

"Can I have a Mickey Mouse telephone?"

"Sure." Alice fingered the money in her pockets. She had separated it, just in case: bills stuffed in each pocket, bills in her purse, a couple in her shoes. "What do you need a phone for?"

"I don't know. I want one."

John Alveira was waiting at the front entrance. She felt a rush of pleasure at the sight of him. He was slouched against the wall, wearing a white shirt with rolled-up sleeves that looked extra bright against his olive skin. She wished she were dressed up!

"Hi! This is my little brother Jamie."

Jamie drew himself up. "Call me Jim."

"Hey, Jim." Alice loved the way John smiled at him, with his eyes crinkling. There was a camera slung over his shoulder.

"You brought a camera?" Alice said.

"Busman's holiday. I might take some shots of you." He grinned. "Just in case you're photogenic." He ruffled her hair and she warmed at his touch. "Why did you spray it?"

"It's just a tiny bit of Tenex."

She felt him messing it up. "Today's your day off, Alice." He looked at her critically. "That's better."

They went into the store and Alice saw herself in one of the mirrored columns. No one would take her for a model now, that was for sure.

Jamie was darting this way and that, touching things at the jewelry counter.

"Look! They got Swatches!"

"You can't even tell time yet."

"So?"

"Jamie, don't touch everything." She was walking quietly next to John.

"Oh, let him," John said.

"I'll race you to the escalator!"

"No, Jamie, you can't—"

"Race him," John said. "I'll follow along."

She looked up at him. What did he want her acting like a kid for? But then she had to go after Jamie so he wouldn't get lost in the crowd.

Jamie went up the escalator and then tried walking down the wrong way, laughing. "Come on, Alice!" They used to do that when she was a kid, to see if they could beat the moving stairs.

"Go ahead," John said. "See if you can do it."

She took a tentative step down and then got in the spirit of it, ignoring the dirty looks around her, and she and Jamie got halfway down before they were carried up again. John was laughing, egging them on. Alice laughed too, dimly aware that he was taking pictures.

"Okay, gang, where to?"

"I don't know. I thought maybe I'd get some skirts and . . ."

She looked at the colorful display of clothing before her.

193

"How about the designer floor? Two flights up," John said.

The *designer* floor. Alice took a breath. Why not?

The fourth floor was arranged in sections separated by mirrored walls. Calvin Klein. Ellen Tracy. Soft beige carpeting. Armani. Jamie ran around the walls, almost into a mirror, and back to Alice.

Ralph Lauren. Norma Kamali. Charles Jourdan.

"Hey, look at this!" There was a top covered with bugle beads, glittering in shades of pink from rose to very pale. Gee, she could wear that at the Gilded Cave! She turned it, letting the light hit and making it sparkle.

"Try it on," John said.

"No, it's Large. I'd need Small."

"Try it on anyway."

She slipped it over her T-shirt and checked in the mirror. It was way too big, hanging limply on her, and looked dumb with jeans and sneakers, but in the right size . . . Why in the world was John taking a picture?

"May I help you?" A saleswoman approached them frostily.

"It's nice, isn't it?" Alice said to John, and then to the saleswoman, "Do you have it in 'Small'?"

"No," she said and hastily took it from her. Hey, lady, Alice thought, my hands aren't dirty.

"Wait a minute. What about over there?" Alice said, indicating a rack where several were hanging.

The saleswoman's cold glance swept over Alice. "This tunic is five hundred and seventy-five dollars," she said dismissively.

"Hey, lady!" Alice said. She furiously shoved her hand in her pocket and came up with a roll of bills. "My green's as good as anyone else's. I want to see it in 'Small'."

194

The saleswoman stared at Alice and then at John. "I might have one left."

"Fine," Alice said haughtily. "Wrap it up."

The transaction was completed and they retrieved Jamie from behind a mirrored wall where he was playing hide-and-seek. Then she saw a bright red silk dress with puffy sleeves and a whole lot of very expensive stuff that was very ugly and a big fuchsia shirt that might be nice . . . and a gray lace dress that she'd consider . . . and a soft white knit. . . . This was pure joy!

She went from rack to rack and there were so many colors and different looks. There was nothing to go with the bugle-beaded tunic. She carried an armload of things into the dressing room and she tried on a lot of stuff and became confused about what she wanted to look like, and after a while, zipping in and out of things seemed like work. She felt almost feverish, like at those kid birthday parties when she'd had too much sugar icing and soda and too many games. Anyway, Iris would know where to get everything wholesale.

They rode up the escalator and Alice looked down at the displays below her. She was on top of the world! They went all the way up to the eighth floor and looked at model rooms. She wanted to buy things for the apartment and didn't know where to start.

"Do you think anyone ever buys the whole room, every single thing in it?"

"Most probably somebody does," John said.

"Your loft's great," she said, "but kind of empty. Don't you want to put more in it? There's not even paintings on the walls. And a rug like that one would look nice."

"I don't like to get bogged down," he said. "I like to be free to pick up and go in a minute."

"Go where?"

He shrugged. "I've thought about breaking away. I've had it with the fashion scene."

"What do you want instead?"

"Well, I've been working on a photo essay that's the most satisfying thing I've done in years. A friend of mine is a journalist and we've been talking about doing something together. I don't know, along the lines of 'Children Under Stress'."

"Meaning what?"

"Okay, bad title. Something about kids under pressure, hothouse-forced into adult situations, lost childhood. . . . He's in Japan now and I thought I might join him."

She felt a stab of dismay. "You're not going to Japan, are you?"

"What's interesting in Japan is the extreme competition in the educational system. By thirteen, kids are either prepping for one of four universities or their future is menial jobs. And the pressure is intense. A lot of kids that make it are burned out, and some of those who don't are suicides. . . . I think that fits in with the theme."

"How are you going to photograph that? You're not going to hang around waiting for a suicide, are you?"

"No. I don't hope for disasters." He sounded offended. "I shoot whatever opportunity presents itself."

"You're not *really* going to Japan?"

"And then we were talking about Belfast, the pressure that kind of situation puts on kids. . . ."

"I just can't believe you'd give up everything." He couldn't really go! It had to be just talk.

"I don't know," he said. "It's a risk."

"Well, you've been working on some project right here in New York, haven't you? What's that about?"

He hesitated. "It's not quite finished."

"You can't go!" she burst out. When he looked at her, surprised, she smiled. "Susan would be *devastated*."

"Very funny."

They went from floor to floor. Cut crystal and gleaming silver, suedes and reptiles, chrome and thick coarse-woven cloth, velvet and lace, midnight blacks and celestial blues. Everything was hers for the taking! She found a Mickey Mouse phone for Jamie, and he was running in circles, flushed with excitement. She bought white satin sheets and a cute heart-shaped pillow.

She dashed through the china department and saw a little ceramic rabbit nibbling a carrot.

"Oh, I want that!"

"That's Royal Copenhagen, miss."

"I'll take it."

She'd start a whole collection of china rabbits. Maybe to put on the mantel, if they had a fireplace. She told the salesman to wrap it in lots of paper, so it wouldn't break.

On the ground floor, she drifted through the perfumes, John and Jamie in her wake. She sprayed her wrists with a cacophony of musk, jasmine, tuberose, Oriental spice. There was one in a pretty crystal bottle that smelled like vanilla. It was wonderful. She extended her arm for John to sniff.

He shook his head. "I'll pass. Makes me sneeze."

"Oh, but this is wonderful. I think I'll—"

"Wait, Alice. You're the Mayhem girl."

"Oh, right. I bet they'll send me a case." She put down the bottle regretfully. "You know something? I don't even know what it smells like."

The ground floor was crowded as they worked their way to the exit. A lady stepped on Jamie's foot and he yelled "Ouch!"

"Wherever I am," Alice said, "it's . . . MAYHEM!"

Then they were out of the air-conditioning, and the heat of the street made Alice wilt. Even John, laden with packages, looked worn out. But Jamie had renewed energy, running back and forth in front of them. "To the bike store! To the bike store!"

Alice linked her arm through John's. This was so good. He was her best friend; she could talk to him about anything. Well, except for the one thing most on her mind—and that was John Alveira.

The store on Third Avenue had bicycles in all sizes and colors.

"You can have any one you want," Alice said grandly. "Any color, any make."

"A ten-speed blue Schwinn!" Jamie said.

The salesman brought it out and put Jamie on it to check the size. Jamie looked at the bike beneath him and then at Alice. His hand stroked the handlebar. His eyes were round and shining, his mouth parted in a tremulous O. Alice could see him through John's eyes: a moment of wonder, frozen in time. She took the packages from John, and John snapped the picture.

"I want a copy of that," Alice said, loving Jamie, loving that she had been able to put that look on his face.

They picked training wheels and a basket and a loud horn. John found a little license plate with JIM on it. He gave it to Jamie with a flourish and said, "My treat." They waited while the accessories were attached. Then, with Jamie seated and clutching the handlebar, they carefully, arduously guided the bicycle over the sidewalks toward home. Jamie was very quiet—awed and exhausted.

"The 'too much, too soon' syndrome," John said, smiling.

"That's a crock!" Alice said. "There's no such thing as too much, too soon. There's only too little and not soon enough."

22

"Boy, with everything that's happening, I'd think you'd be a little happy!" Alice looked at Claire with exasperation. Claire's high had peaked and she was way down in one of her lows. You'd think with everything going so well, she'd snap right out of it.

Claire hadn't even gotten dressed and it was late afternoon. She was still in her raggedy beige nightgown, staring blankly at nothing, sipping her glass of Beaujolais—never enough to get drunk, just enough to soften the edges. She hadn't even roused herself to go looking for an apartment!

"You *wanted* to move!"

"I'll get to it," Claire said tonelessly.

Even when Alice tried on the glittering tunic from Bloomingdale's, Claire didn't react.

"What's the *matter* with you, Ma?"

Claire looked for an answer in the rose liquid. "I had my dreams, too, you know," she finally said.

So it was up to Alice to find an apartment and it wasn't easy, with all the other things she had to do. She was going to save all day Sunday for serious looking, but then Jamie pleaded with her to take him out on the bike.

"How'm I gonna learn to ride it if I can't *ride* it?"

"Okay, but just for the morning."

They struggled to get it down the stairs and Alice let him ride along the sidewalk, ignoring the annoyance of the pedestrians who had to dodge out of the way. They headed west toward the park. Central Park was closed to traffic on Sundays and they went to the Fifty-ninth Street Drive. Jamie pumped determinedly as other bicycles whizzed by. Alice jogged alongside.

"See! I know how!"

"You're doing good, Jamie."

"Can we take the training wheels off?"

"Not yet. That's a lot harder."

"I want to try! Come on, I want to try!"

She unscrewed the training wheels and he wobbled precariously and tipped to the side. He couldn't balance. He watched other riders race past, crushed with disappointment.

"Don't worry, you'll catch on," Alice said.

She took a ride. The trees and grass smelled good and, for once, it wasn't muggy. She could have gone on riding and riding, the breeze ruffling her hair. She hadn't done anything like that in a long time. She felt free, free of all responsibility,

201

riding with the wind. . . . She turned back to Jamie and re-placed the training wheels.

"I'll practice so hard!" His legs churned as he tried to pick up speed. He grinned as he went way ahead of her.

When it was time to go, he begged, "Five more minutes."

"No, I've got things to do. You want a new apartment, don't you?"

"Three more?"

"We'll come back here another time."

"Three *seconds?*"

She laughed. It was nice to see his face so eager, framed by the green of the park. "Let's go. You can ride all the way home." They went back along the sidewalks.

"I'll practice every single day. I know where to go."

"Don't even think of taking it out by yourself," Alice said. "There's too much traffic."

"I'll go on the sidewalk."

"You can't cross with a bike, not by yourself."

"I'll wait for the green light."

"No. You wait for me to take you. Promise me, Jamie."

"When? You're always *busy.*"

"Anyway, you couldn't get it down the stairs by yourself."

"I could too."

"You can go with Ma. I'll tell her to take you." Claire could do that much.

"How come you're always working? Do you like it?"

"Mostly, it's boring," Alice said. "There's a lot of waiting around." If she had to squeeze in apartment hunting on top of everything else, Claire could at least do something for Jamie.

The Mayhem TV commercial was on the air often. It was exciting to see it with the music and special effects. Then the September issue of *Vogue* came out in August and the fur pictures were in it. Of all the poses from that long, long shoot, they had only used three with Alice in them, but still . . . The Mayhem print ad ran in a whole lot of places: *The New York Times Magazine, Mademoiselle, Cosmopolitan*. . . . Partly because of the exposure, Billie was getting a lot of calls for Alice—next week, a shoot for a jewelry company, a major fashion show, and a Lorline lipstick print ad. It was a good thing all those jobs were coming in. The more money she made, the faster it seemed to be going out. She wasn't going back to school in the fall, so she'd have to hire a tutor—that was the law—and it wouldn't be cheap. And Iris said the curvy look was coming back and that Alice ought to have silicone breast implants. That would be four thousand dollars. She hated the idea of someone cutting her, but then she could do bathing suits and lingerie. . . . She had to have manicures and pedicures and Damian doing her hair. Claire had quit Office Temporaries and they sure weren't eligible for welfare anymore, so there were all the everyday things like food and clothing and cabs. Once Alice got used to wearing *good* clothes, she couldn't go back to the bargain stuff. And all the rental agents wanted a whole lot of money up front. Finally, with Iris vouching for her—she was Alice Lonner, the Mayhem girl, after all—she found a place where they were willing to wait for the security deposit.

The building was on East Sixty-second Street, not too far from the old place and Jamie's school, but closer to Madison Avenue. There was a uniformed doorman and a marble lobby filled with plants, and Alice liked it even before she saw the apartment.

She walked through the three empty bedrooms, her high heels clicking on freshly scraped oak floors. Three bedrooms. *Two* bathrooms, and one had a stall shower. She looked out the window and the view was mostly just the buildings across the street, but it was great anyway! She liked the fresh wood smell and the just-painted white walls; it was bare and clean and full of possibilities. She took a deep breath and said, "I'll take it."

The day they moved in, the apartment lost some of its brand-new look. Their shabby furniture looked matchbox-rickety in the vast space. It was only temporary, Alice thought, just until she had time to order new things. She'd seen some terrific pale leather pieces in an ad. She couldn't wait to throw out the stained, lumpy couch and the scratched-up, peeling table.

That night, she closed the door of her bedroom to shut out the sounds of Claire and Jamie. Her bedroom was empty except for the bed. She made it with the white satin sheets. She carefully placed the white china rabbit on the windowsill and surveyed her realm. For the first time in her life, she had a space of her own. It was exactly what she wanted, uncluttered and private. The satin sheets glimmered luxuriously.

It was getting late and she watched lights blinking off in windows across the street. She stroked the china rabbit, nibbling its little orange carrot. It wasn't the kind of thing she could take to sleep with her.

She got into bed. The satin sheets were cold and slippery. The air conditioner hummed noisily and she jumped up to turn it off. She reminded herself of how good it was to feel a little chilly when the night outside was hot and humid. Back in bed, she closed her eyes and, in a little while, opened them again. Her body ached from the long day of packing and unpacking. She thought of her pretty new clothes, hanging uncrowded in the immaculate closet. Its mirrored door reflected the dim light from the window. If she didn't get to sleep soon, her eyes would look terrible for the session scheduled in the morning.

The more she willed herself into sleep, the more wide awake she became, overwhelmed by the unfamiliarity of the refrigerator-white room.

Finally, she got up and opened her door. All the lights were out. Her bare feet were silent on the polished wood floor as she moved into the hall. She heard Claire's bed creaking. She tiptoed to the open door of Jamie's room and listened to his deep, even breathing. Silently, she moved closer to his bed. He was burrowed under the covers, his mouth partly open. She gently nudged him aside and eased under the blanket. He murmured quietly in his sleep. She tucked herself next to him, spoon fashion, next to the sleepy warmth of his body. His hair smelled of soap and bubble gum. She breathed in unison with him and drifted into sleep.

23

Alice got into the habit of dropping into John Alveira's loft often, if she was in the neighborhood—or even if she wasn't. If he was out, she'd leave a note on the door—a smiley face and, "Alice Lonner was here," or, "The Mayhem Girl strikes again." If he was in, she'd hang out and watch him work and sometimes pick up something from the Italian deli downstairs.

Toward the end of August, she was busier than ever, so she hadn't been there for more than a week. She rang downstairs and was happy to see his face appear at the window.

"Hi. Come on up!"

He let her into the loft. "What've you been up to? I missed you."

She smiled triumphantly. "You missed me, huh? You missed me!"

"Well, not really," he said. "I got used to someone underfoot. Felt strange with no one around to bug me."

"You could call me sometime," she said. "You could take me out, you know."

"I'm not into robbing the cradle, Alice."

She made a face at him.

"Okay. I owe you dinner for all those deli sandwiches."

Her eyes lit up. "Would you? Take me out to dinner sometime?"

"Sure, why not?"

"Let's go someplace romantic! With candles and roses and a very private corner and—"

"And you'll peel me a grape?" He laughed.

"What's so funny?" she said. "Hey John, is there something *wrong* with me?" She was beautiful, everybody said so. "How old do I have to be?"

"At the age of reason, brat. Come into the darkroom, I'm right in the middle of—"

"What are you working on?"

"Gloves. Great social significance."

She liked the darkroom, the familiar vinegary smell, the dimness of the red safety light. She looked at the negative projected on the base of the enlarger. Two gloved hands in reverse color, white for black, a bracelet around one wrist.

"That's nice! The way that finger points and—"

"Watch this." He moved the black frame. "See what a difference cropping makes?" He had cut out most of the wrist, leaving the bracelet framing one end of the photograph.

She looked at it critically. "Because the hands are more dramatic when they're not centered?"

"Right. That's good, Alice."

"I was taking graphic art in school and—"

"Design Trades, I forgot. Hand me some matte paper. On the middle shelf." He positioned the sheet of paper under the enlarger and exposed it. "Do you think you'll miss school?"

She shrugged. "Modeling's better, I guess."

"It won't last forever."

"Oh, I've got years and years."

"You never know. You could get overexposed; this is a business that eats up new faces. You're bright. You should be learning something."

"I'm learning about modeling."

"Don't strain your brain, kid."

He dipped the exposed paper into developer and they watched the image swim into view. Then into stopper and hypo.

"A model isn't just a pretty face. Models have to project personality," Alice said, quoting Iris.

"True," he said, "but that doesn't exactly add up to a major education."

"What do you care?" Alice said defensively.

"I do care, Alice. I care." He looked at her, then quickly looked away. He hung the photograph on the drying rack.

"Well, I'm learning about photography."

"You ready to take over from me?"

"You know that Diane Arbus book, the one you have next to Ansel Adams? I was looking through it."

"Mmm-hmm."

"She makes everyone look grotesque."

"That was her view of the world. A photographer communicates his view—that is, if he's not working on gloves."

"Well, there are good gloves and bad gloves."

"And I do damn good gloves." He smiled. "You're a good kid."

"It's not fair!"

"What isn't?"

"Diane Arbus. Those were real people. Did she *ask* them if they wanted to look grotesque?"

He shrugged. "Maybe she was just recording them as they were."

"A photographer can twist things. You said yourself, it's all in his point of view."

He switched on the light and Alice blinked. He stretched. "That's it for now."

She followed him into the living area. "Can I see your pictures of Magdalena?"

"How about something to eat? You want to run down?"

"Why can't I see them? Come on, John."

"What for? There's no point—"

"She was a great model. I'd like to see."

"They're just photographs. No big deal. You know the big cabinet in the darkroom? Magdalena's filed under 'M'. Help yourself."

She went back into the darkroom and riffled through the file folders. "Is that the way you do it? Just alphabetically?" she called to him.

"It's as good a system as any," he called back.

"I thought you'd have something more complicated." Magdalena had a group of folders devoted to her. The first one she opened had a bunch of fashion poses and included the picture on Iris's wall. Another one contained more candid shots. She took that one back into the living area with her.

She noticed that John had poured himself a shot.

She sat cross-legged on the couch, her suede pants stretched taut. Slowly, she studied each photograph. Magdalena in a kitchen, a kerchief tied around her head, stirring something in a pot, radiant smile. Magdalena at a window with filmy curtains, soft focus, in profile, a thoughtful, almost sad expression. Magdalena, looking elegant even in a terrycloth bathrobe, hair wet, droplets of water running down the sculptured face. Magdalena asleep, serene, on a flowered pillow. These weren't fashion shots. These were personal—too personal.

Alice glanced up at John. He didn't meet her eyes; he was busy lighting a cigarette.

What kind of personality was coming through the photographs? She looked proud and warm and worldly, and obviously bathed in a glow of love. The photographer's point of view was no mystery. Alice felt simple and unpolished in comparison.

"You loved her a lot."

"Yes. Look, I was twenty-one years old. She made a big impression."

Alice hesitated painfully before she spoke. "Do you still love her?"

He laughed. "The last time I saw her was almost ten years ago. You don't love someone in absentia for ten years."

"Thinking about her makes you sad, though."

"Sad? Not so much about Maggie. Mostly, it's remembering the way *I* was."

"How do you mean?"

"I guess it's thinking about how young I was and the potential I had then. . . ."

"But you're very successful!"

"Not exactly the way I wanted to be."

Alice looked at a full-length shot of Magdalena in boots and pants, romping with a collie.

"How old was she, in this one?"

"That one? Thirty-four."

"You were thirteen years apart! You didn't think that was too much, did you?"

"That was different. . . . And maybe that was one of the things that went wrong. I can understand how she felt."

"I'm going to be fifteen in October."

"Happy birthday."

"Fifteen from thirty-one is only sixteen."

"You can still subtract. Who said models were dumb?"

"Won't you even *talk* about it?"

"No. Hey, I've got a job this afternoon, so . . ."

"I know you're straight, right?"

He shook his head incredulously. "Yeah, at last glance."

"Then I don't understand why you won't—"

"Alice, this is all very flattering, but—"

"I'm the Mayhem girl! I'm exciting and glamorous and sexy! How can you resist me?"

"Don't start believing your press, kiddo."

"We have fun together," Alice said.

"We're friends," he said.

"That's not all," Alice said. "Is it?"

He sat down next to her on the couch and took her shoulders in his hands. He looked her straight in the face, very seriously. "Alice, listen to me. Don't make it tough. Yes, you're beautiful. And fun. And bright. You're going to be one hell of a woman one day. The point is, you're not a woman yet and I don't want to stunt your growth. I don't want that responsibility."

She looked at him carefully. He looked so pained.

"When I'm twenty, you'll only be thirty-six. That doesn't sound so far apart."

"No." They looked into each other's eyes and then he got up quickly, breaking the mood. "So give me a call when you're twenty," he said lightly.

It was the Midsummer's Eve AIDS Benefit and Ball, and the entire fashion industry had assembled to take care of its own. It started because of the death of renowned designer, Charles Erte. First, there was idle talk of a benefit for AIDS research, and then, Jerry Cramer, who was masculine beyond a doubt, put his prestige behind the idea. When everyone else had jumped on the bandwagon, when it was absolutely safe and fashionable, Iris Martin bought a table.

Alice was awed by the beauty of the ballroom. Crystal chandeliers sparkled, and sputtering white candles glowed everywhere. Each table was covered with a white moiré cloth, topped with sprays of baby's breath, white lilacs, and multicolored lilies. Garlands of brightly ribboned flowers ran along the walls under gold molding. It was romantic and opulent—and it was real. This was not another setting for a commercial, Alice thought. She was here in real life.

"Everyone will be there. . . . it's a super chance for you to be seen," Billie had said.

Alice wore a flamenco-style dress that Damian had helped her choose. It had a strapless bustier of scarlet silk that exploded at her hips into three swirling, ruffled skirts, one of fuchsia layered between two of black silk organza. It was the first floor-length dress she had ever worn outside of work. She was grateful for the fashion show experience that had taught her how to maneuver in it and on the delicate high heels. The only thing missing was diamonds. Anything less seemed wrong, so Alice wore no jewelry at all. Instead, she wore a huge scarlet silk rose in her hair.

Alice sipped champagne and wandered through the crowded room, inhaling the warm, spicy fragrance of Mayhem that surrounded her. The band was playing and a myriad of colors whirled on the floor. The fashion industry sure knew how to do things with style.

Kerstin and Jessica were there, too, and it was fun to talk to them again. Oscar de la Renta was there, and Calvin Klein, and Grace Mirabella, and she caught a glimpse of Diane von Furstenburg chatting with Carol Alt. And—incredibly—they knew who *she* was.

"You could be arrested for looking that hot." The familiar deep voice made her whirl around. John Alveira! John, terribly handsome in a dinner jacket.

"Hi."

He looked her over. "Sensational, effective as hell."

She smiled happily. "It's a Valentino! I got it whole-sale."

"Well, I'm glad you're not spending like a drunken sailor anymore." He laughed.

"You look pretty nice yourself," she said. "I've never seen you *dressed*."

"Ssshhh," he said. "We don't want the whole world to know."

"Everything is so—" She gestured widely."—so beauti-ful!"

"Look around you. Everyone's working the room."

"Working the room?"

"Pressing hands, making contacts. Aside from the good cause, that's what they're here for. Business as usual."

"No, it's romantic and beautiful! Is that the *waltz* they're doing?"

He nodded.

"I wish I knew how."

"Come on, it's not hard."

She gulped the remains of her champagne and put the glass on a passing tray. He whirled her around and around. The sparkling crystal above her became a blur.

They parted when the first course was served and she returned to Iris's table. She was introduced to a million people and she said "hi" to a million more. And throughout the evening, she and John came together and parted, like figures in a vast minuet.

She saw him at a distance, downing shots and laughing with

a group. Then he was close, his arm around her, and she was light-headed and giddy. She felt wonderful!

There were speeches and more champagne and chocolate mousse and more champagne and John Alveira. John Alveira. Iris pushed her to meet some designers and they *loved* her.

She was whirled away again and Kerstin giggled and whispered something in her ear and a man with a mustache sniffed the rose in her hair and said, "Delicious!" And the evening wound down long before she was ready to go.

"Come on," John said. "I'll take you home."

"I hate to leave. . . ."

"You'll turn into a pumpkin."

"Mayhem girls don't turn into pumpkins!"

"Let's go, Alice."

"It was *so* nice. I *love* champagne."

"You loved it a little too much tonight."

"Oh, no! I feel . . . magnificent!"

"You'll have a magnificent head in the morning."

In the cab, she snuggled against him and leaned her head on his shoulder. "You should be more mature, John."

"What?"

"About accepting people for what they are."

"What are you talking about?"

She frowned with concentration to get the words right. "It's unfair to judge a person by her age. No one else here does. You're practicing ageism, John."

He laughed. "There's something wrong with your logic somewhere."

"Where?"

He shook his head to clear it. "Offhand, I don't know."

"See!" she said triumphantly.

She tilted her head up and looked at him, her lips a breath away. He looked at her and a long moment passed and then his lips were on hers.

24

Jamie had been up for hours. He kept his eye on the door of Alice's room, waiting for her to come out. And then she came out with that makeup bag. Shoot, that meant she was going to work. He'd been hoping to go bike-riding today. She had said Sunday and then she'd slept way past lunchtime, on account of she'd been to a Midsummer till dawn, and they didn't go. So he thought maybe today. What did she have all that stuff in her bag for anyway? He didn't even like the way she looked with all that stuff on her face.

"Morning, Jamie."

"Are you working today?"

"Yeah, and I'd better get moving."

"Can you take me out on the bike later?"

"No. I've got a lipstick ad and that'll take hours."

"This afternoon?"

"I said no. I don't know when I'll get home. . . . Did you have breakfast?"

He'd had two Devil Dogs. She wouldn't like that. He looked away.

"Get yourself some cereal, okay? I've got to run."

"But what about—"

"I can't be late." She was pulling that big bag over her shoulder. "Hey, I'm sorry about yesterday—maybe next weekend."

"I want to ride my bike *today*."

"Ma will be up soon. Ask her, okay?"

"Okay."

"So long."

"Alice?"

"See you later, Jamie." She was out the door in a flash.

Ma wouldn't be up for a long time. Anyway, Ma wouldn't go anywhere. She had the blues. He had heard her and Alice talking.

"You ought to see someone," Alice had said. "I heard there's medicine that—"

"I'm not sick," Claire had said. "I've just got the blues."

Jamie turned on the TV and watched cartoons for a while. Then he did karate kicks all around the living room. Then there was nothing to do.

How was he going to ride like the big kids if he didn't practice? He didn't want training wheels forever and ever. He went into his room and sat down on the bike. He held the handlebars. He rode it a tiny little way and bumped right into the wall. It made a mark; Alice would get mad. Riding in the park was fun. He knew the way, too. He knew just how to go. He'd go on the sidewalks and he'd wait for the green lights. He knew how. Alice thought he was a baby!

He wheeled the bike out of his room and to the front door. Alice had said "no." Alice had said "promise me." But he didn't cross-his-heart-and-hope-to-die. Alice said he couldn't get the bike down the stairs by himself. But now they had an elevator! He could do it!

He went back to his room and put on his brand new Surfers' Alliance T-shirt and tucked his GI Joe membership card in his jeans pocket. Now he looked cool. The bike was waiting for him at the door, just like a trusty steed.

The elevator door kept trying to close, but he held it open and he pushed the bike in and it just fit. He wheeled it through the big lobby. The doorman opened the door.

"Goin' for a turn around the block, are you?"

"Yes, sir," Jamie said.

He rode the bicycle on the sidewalk and stopped at the corner. He waited for the light to change and he walked it across to the other side of the street in plenty of time. Then there was another block and another.

"Watch out, sonny!" a man said nastily. He wasn't even in his way! He didn't like anyone calling him sonny. He was going to tell everyone to call him Jim. Alice's friend with the camera called him Jim.

Another block and he got tired of getting off and on the bike at each crossing. He stayed on and looked both ways *very* carefully and bumped it off the curb. A cab was making a right turn, but it stopped for him and he got across in plenty of time. He felt proud of himself. Riding a bike across the street wasn't so hard. Anyway, Alice was always bossing him around and she was only his *sister*. She wasn't that old; she didn't know everything. He'd tell her tonight that he'd gone all by himself.

It was very hot. It would be better in the park. He'd ride so fast he'd make his own breeze. He'd ride so fast! He saw the green of the park. He was almost there. Then he was riding on Fifth Avenue, alongside the park wall. The sun made him squint. There was the 59th Street Drive! He'd made it!

He went barreling right onto the drive—and there were CARS! He was in the middle of traffic! A car horn honked. The cars were whizzing by and there was no place to stop and turn around. They allowed cars on the drive on Mondays! There was hardly any room for him on the side. He couldn't go back. A horn honked loud behind him and he pedaled as fast as he could. He was so scared. More horns honked. He was SCARED! His eyes blurred with tears. Then there was a BUMP. He felt his hands torn off the handlebars. Mama! Alice! He never felt his head hit the curb.

25

Lorline's new makeup promotion was the Medieval Magic line. Alice's lips were covered with Primitive Bronze and they had dressed her in chain mail. The metal felt icy against her bare chest. The session was especially long. A hooded hawk was placed on her shoulder and she felt its talons digging in. Its agitated movements made her nervous. The chain mail wouldn't drape properly and finally the stylist stapled it together at Alice's back. She was working on her "fierce" look when she heard the message.

"Miss Lonner's booker is on the phone," an assistant whispered.

"For God's sake, not *now!*" the photographer exploded as the assistant shrank back.

"Tell her I'll call at the next break," Alice said. It wasn't like Billie to interrupt a job. She was probably super-enthusiastic about something; maybe the Italian fashion showings had come through.

They went back to work. Head held high. Click. Flared nostrils. Click. Alice was relieved when the hawk was removed. She thought the Lorline ads were getting sillier and sillier; it was a good thing they hadn't *welded* her in. Her face was covered with chalky white paste and her eyelids were black. And who was making up these names, anyway? Primitive Bronze, Legendary Scarlet, Guinevere Rose. Well, luckily, her look was just what they wanted. She smiled, head tilted back. Click. She worked easily with this photographer, with a minimum of instructions.

"Excuse me." The assistant came in hesitantly. "Miss Lonner's booker called again."

"What is it?" The photographer sounded exasperated.

"Miss Lonner, she said to tell you—uh—there's been an accident. Your brother."

Jamie. Jamie! "What happened? Where?"

"She said to tell you—the Emergency Room at St. Luke's —"

Alice struggled with the chain mail. "Get me out of this!"

"Alice, wait, can't we finish here and—"

"Somebody, please!" She was pulling at it frantically.

"It's probably nothing, why don't you call first and—"

"We're almost finished, Alice, couldn't you wait until—"

"Get me out of this or I'll tear it apart, I swear to God I will!" Alice felt the pulse pounding in her forehead.

The stylist was all thumbs with the pliers. It was taking much too long.

222

"Did Billie say what happened?" Alice asked. She tried to brush away the horrifying images in her mind.

"No," the assistant said, "just to tell you they want you in the Emergency Room."

"Where's St. Luke's?" Alice heard the faint scrape of the metal links under the stylist's fingers.

"St. Luke's—Roosevelt. On Ninth Ave," the photographer said. "Anyone know the street?"

"59th or 60th," the hairdresser said. "A cabbie would know."

"Oh, please, get me out of this," Alice said through gritted teeth. There was a crawling, icy sensation on her bare skin.

"Someone, call a cab for her!" the stylist said.

Alice pulled free of the chain mail and threw on her jeans and T-shirt with shaking hands. She streaked out of the studio and down the hall to the exit, the photographer's voice trailing behind her.

"It's probably nothing, Alice," he was saying, "A bad nosebleed or a twisted ankle, you know, kids that age . . ."

She knew, though. She knew it was bad. Claire wouldn't take him to a hospital unless she absolutely had to.

First she saw Claire's face, pale and strained. Then Jamie, quiet and very little, lying on a makeshift cot. The faint smells of disinfectant and adhesive filled the small cubicle.

"Ma?"

"He was thrown off the bike. It's a concussion. Oh, I'm so glad you're here, Alice."

"A concussion? What's happening now?"

"They're calling someone to do a CAT scan. . . . Oh, Alice. . . ."

A green-gowned attendant leaned into the cubicle. "Try to wake him," he said.

"Wake him?" Alice repeated. "How?"

"Talk to him. Keep talking to him." The puzzled way the attendant was looking at her made her aware that she was still in full makeup, complete with inch-long eyelashes. "See if you can keep him awake."

"Jamie?" Alice leaned over him. His eyes flickered under the lids. "Jamie? It's Alice. Jamie?" Nothing. She gently shook his shoulder. "Jamie, wake up."

His eyes opened and looked at her vacantly. He twisted his shoulder away. "No! Don't, Dad!"

Dad? She felt a sinking sensation in her stomach. He was back long ago, when his father was still with them. He shrank under her touch.

"Jamie—"

"No! I didn't do it!" He moved away from her.

"Jamie, it's me. Alice."

His eyes stared at her, empty; he wasn't there at all. His face was a shell.

"Jamie, wake up."

The wide open eyes stared at her, expressionless. Where was he?

Alice looked at Claire. Claire was crying softly, her face frightened. Claire was no good at all to either of them.

She felt icy calm, aware of the attendant in the entrance of the cubicle, aware of a telephone ringing down the hall, aware of Jamie sliding back into unconsciousness. "Jamie, I'm here." And suddenly her knees weren't holding her and she was sinking down. A brown arm held her up.

"Here, take a deep breath." The fumes of ammonia cleared her head and made her eyes sting.

"I'm sorry," she said, ashamed.

"Hey, you're entitled. Are you all right?"

"Yes."

He handed her the cotton pad with ammonia on it. "Hold on to this, okay?"

She heard Claire's voice. "Jamie, it's Mommy."

"Where's a doctor?" Alice said.

"They'll be taking him up for the CAT scan in a minute." He patted her arm and left.

"Jamie, wake up," she said. His eyelids fluttered and closed. She saw the large wet stain on his jeans, deep blue against the light blue. Poor Jamie, he'd be so embarrassed when he woke up. When he woke up. He was all wet and he had to be cold. Could she get those pants off? Was it all right to move him?

She saw a nurse passing in the hall. "Nurse! Please . . . my brother's pants are all wet. . . ."

"That happens, with the shock," the nurse said. "The whole body just lets go."

"Could someone change him or . . . is there a hospital gown or . . ."

"You can take off his things. I'll find a blanket for you somewhere."

Alice unzipped the fly. She kept her hand from shaking. She was afraid to jostle him too much while she pulled off the jeans. "Ma, help me." Claire held his legs up while she pulled off the underpants. There was a strong odor of stale urine. Jamie would hate this so much; this was such an invasion of his little-boy dignity.

225

Claire was holding the clothes. "What should we do with this?"

"I don't know. Throw them in there." There was a metal pail on the floor. "Jamie?" His skin felt icy cold. "Jamie, wake up."

She stalked to the doorway and called down the hall, "We need a blanket here! My little brother's freezing!"

A nurse brought in a rough wool blanket and Alice doubled it and covered him. His face was waxy against the navy blue.

"I've been trying to wake him," Alice said, "but he opens his eyes and . . ." She felt weak-kneed again and wished she knew what she had done with that cotton pad of ammonia. ". . . and it's like . . . his personality is gone."

"That happens sometimes with a concussion," the nurse said.

Oh, please, Alice thought, please let Jamie come back. She hated forcing him awake and having him twist away from her.

"Maybe we should let him sleep?" Claire asked. "Let him rest?"

"It's better to try to keep him awake," the nurse said. "Anyway, he'll be taken up for the CAT scan in just a moment."

"What is that?" Alice asked.

"A very sophisticated X ray to check for any internal injury. He took quite a blow to the head."

Claire whimpered.

"Just a routine procedure," the nurse said. She left with an encouraging smile.

Alice shook Jamie's shoulder gently. He moaned and opened

his eyes, expressionless and unseeing. Alice felt her insides contract. Come back, Jamie. "Jamie, please." He moaned again and turned away.

Two attendants came and wheeled him down the hall, a whirring sound on the white linoleum floor. Alice watched them turn a corner and go out of sight. The blanket had been pushed up and his leg was exposed. Alice hoped they would cover him.

She and Claire waited side by side on a bench in the hallway. Claire was fidgeting, sniffling, twisting a tissue in her hands. Alice hugged herself tightly and sat immobile. Near them, a man held his hand, blood dripping through the fingers, and moaned. Someone else was wheeled down the hall at a run, wheels clattering on the floor, a nurse running alongside, holding an IV container aloft.

Alice felt the thick makeup caking her face. That chalky paste was hell on the skin, if she didn't get it off soon, what if she broke out— What was wrong with her? How could she think about her skin when Jamie was . . . She was worse than Kerstin with her mosquito bite. Oh, Jamie!

Across the hall, an old lady was praying softly in Spanish. Alice wanted to pray and didn't know where to begin. All that came to mind was a variation on the punchline of one of John Alveira's jokes.

> *Alice:* God, you gave me a roller-coaster mother and a disappearing father. Wasn't that enough? Why are you doing this to me?
> *God:* Oops. Sorry, Alice. I didn't recognize you.

"How did this happen?" Alice asked Claire.

"He took his bike to the 59th Street Drive. I don't know, I never heard him leave. You know something? He had his GI Joe membership card in his pocket; that's how they could identify him and call me. A car sideswiped him."

"Couldn't you have taken him, just once? That's all he wanted, someone to take him bike-riding."

"He never asked me," Claire said.

Alice lost all sense of time. It could have been afternoon, it could have been midnight. Fluorescent tubes replaced daylight and the stale air was punctuated with sounds she associated with TV. "Dr. Klein. Calling Dr. Klein." Faint sound of bells. "Dr. Wendell to the OR."

Then a nurse calling, "Lonner!" and they jumped to their feet. They were met by a young doctor, fatigue etched in his face.

"Mrs. Lonner? I'm Dr. Ray . . ."

"Yes," Claire breathed, "yes, doctor?"

"The scan showed some signs of hemorrhaging on the left side of—"

Claire whimpered.

"What does that mean? Is he all right?" Alice said.

"His condition is stable now. The pressure has been relieved, but it's too early to make a prognosis." The doctor's voice took on a gentler, less official tone. "If there is brain damage . . . we can't assess the extent of the damage until . . ."

"Can't you *do* something?" Alice moaned.

" . . . in cases like this . . . not until he wakes up . . . we don't know at this point . . ."

228

It wasn't fair! Jamie hadn't even seen anything of the world, he didn't know anything, he hadn't had enough time yet!

"Where is he?" Alice said.

"Intensive Care, third floor."

They went up in the elevator and down long winding corridors and through swinging doors. Alice tasted metal in her mouth. Jamie, she thought. I'll take you bike-riding every day. I'll read to you—that Winnie-the-Pooh book I never finished. I'll take you places, anywhere you want. If only . . .

They came to the door of Intensive Care with its No Admittance sign.

If only you come back.

26

They stood in the hallway outside Intensive Care. Claire twisted and turned the tissue in her hand. Long silences were interrupted by occasional footsteps and doors closing.

A nurse came out to speak to them. "He's sleeping. You'll be able to see him in the morning, Mrs. Lonner."

"I want to be here when he wakes up," Alice said.

"It won't be for a while . . . . You should get some rest."

They stood helplessly in the hallway.

"You can't do anything for him now," the nurse said gently. "Go home and sleep for a few hours. . . ." She retreated through the double doors.

"Alice, let's go home and—" Claire said.

"No. You go ahead, Ma."

Home? There'd be Jamie's chair next to the table. She could

see him, picking sausages out of pizza. The living room floor, where he'd lie on his stomach and roll his truck. Jamie, in the bathroom doorway, a smile full of toothpaste. No, she *couldn't* go there. He'd be everywhere and nowhere.

"Come with me, baby."

"No, I don't want to. Go ahead, I'll meet you later."

She watched Claire vanish around a bend of the corridor. She tilted her head back against the wall. The lettering on the gray metal door became blurred. She listened to herself breathing. Hours to wait. She had to get out, get some air.

Outside, it was dark. There were people walking, talking, smiling under the streetlamps. Her legs moved automatically. The peal of someone's laughter pierced her. Headlights blinded her. She had to get away. She hailed a cab.

"Where to?" the driver said.

She hesitated, lost.

"Hey, aren't you that Mayhem girl?"

"Ten Mercer Street," she said, in a voice that made him stare.

She rang and rang the outside bell at John Alveira's. No answer. She rang and rang. Finally, she sagged onto the sidewalk, her back against the wall. She curled her body into a little ball, holding herself tight, her head in her hands.

"Alice?" She looked up. It was John. "We've got to stop meeting like this."

She stared dumbly at him.

"Another emergency, huh? You're out of cab fare again?"

"Jamie," she said. She forced the words out. "Jamie got hurt. His brain."

His face changed. He shook his head, No.

"Please. Help me."

He put his arm around her and led her up to the loft.

"I couldn't go back to the apartment," she mumbled into his chest. "I couldn't."

"Easy, Alice." He lowered her into a sitting position on the couch. "How did . . . he . . . ?"

She faced him, her eyes round and dark. "The bicycle. A car. He was all by himself!"

"No. Oh, Christ!" He lit a cigarette and inhaled deeply.

"They told me to go home. They said it would take hours. . . . John, he was gone. He wasn't there!"

He sat with her as the ashtray overflowed.

"He's all alone." Her throat hurt. "He's still so little. I should be there . . ."

He covered her with a blanket and she dozed, exhausted and dreamless. She started awake, hoping she was coming out of a nightmare, knowing she wasn't.

She saw the first hint of dawn coming through the leaded windows. John was up, smoking and drinking coffee.

"John! How long was I sleeping? I have to go to him!"

"Less than an hour. Does your booker know?"

"No."

"What's her home number?"

"555-4530."

She heard him talking to Billie. "Sorry, did I wake you? . . . I know it's too early. . . . concussion. . . . well, they'll have to cancel the session. . . . I think you'd better put a hold on everything. . . . Okay, I'll tell her. Okay, thanks." The

232

receiver clicked into place. "Billie says to tell you how sorry she is."

"Yeah, I'll bet she's sorry to lose the bookings."

"You're wrong, Alice. She sounded genuinely upset."

"Oh, it's not just Billie, Billie's all right. Everyone wants a piece of me. My mother, Iris, even Rosie, everyone's on line for their cut. Except for you and Jamie. Jamie—" Her hand went up to her mouth. The name came out scratched and torn. "Jamie never wanted anything more than just me, my company."

"Alice, I—"

"I was so busy all the time. So damn *busy!* All the times he watched me run out . . . If I'd been home . . ."

"Don't, Alice. Don't start blaming yourself."

"All that busyness and running around, standing on some guy's chest, saying the same line over and over like a trained parrot—I don't even know what I was doing it for."

"You've had an incredible opportunity. You have to learn how to use it. Exploit it, don't *be* exploited. . . ."

"I want my little brother."

"I wish I knew how to help," he said.

"Just be here for me."

"I will be, as long as I can." He looked away from her. "I told you about my journalist friend in Tokyo, remember? I went to have my passport renewed today. I'm going ahead with that trip to Japan. I can postpone it, but not indefinitely. . . ."

"Oh," she said. "You're really doing it?"

"Yeah, I've finally got it together."

233

"I didn't think you'd really go. I didn't think you'd leave me. . . ."

"It's not *leaving* you. . . . Alice, you can't make more of our . . . friendship . . . than—"

"Because of my age?" She sighed, exhausted. "I'm a million years old."

"I guess you are," he said. He fumbled for a match and lit another cigarette. "Do you want something to eat? Coffee?"

"Okay, coffee."

She moved restlessly to the window. There was a veil of gray over the day. Garbage overflowed the tin cans at the curb and a painfully thin cat rummaged through it. And she remembered Jamie's eyes round and shining, his mouth parted in a tremulous O, at the bicycle store.

"John?" she said, her voice husky. "I want the picture you took of—" Jamie would look like that again, he had to!

"What?" He was running water at the kitchen sink, his back to her. "I can't hear you."

"Never mind. I'll find it." She needed to see it, to hold on to it like a talisman.

"Find what? Instant okay?"

"Yes," she said. She went into the darkroom, to the file cabinets. She remembered his system, simple, alphabetical. *J. Jazz Studies. Jewelry Show. Jordache. Jordan, Elizabeth.* No *Jamie.*

"Need some towels?" she heard him call.

He thought she was in the bathroom. "No. I'll be right there."

Last name, she thought. She pulled out the *L* drawer. *Lake Views. Lancome. Lester, Harold. Lonner, Alice.* There were two thick folders.

There were photos of her and Tanya from that fur shoot. She thumbed through them quickly, searching for the picture of Jamie, frantic now, feeling if she could find it, she could will him back. . . . There was the full-face shot from their first meeting that had been used for the agency headsheet. She riffled quickly through others from that session—and then her hand stopped. There was a picture of her, waif-like, bare-faced, hair slicked back, wolfing down a sandwich, her cheeks puffed with food. She felt a wave of shock and embarrassment; it looked like an ad for "Save the Children"! With numb disbelief, she took in the others. A photo of her on John's couch, Kerstin's suede camisole half-unlaced, exposing a skinny chest, caked makeup, and smudged eyeshadow. One from Bloomingdale's, a fistful of bills in her hand, an ugly snarl at the saleswoman. She and Jamie going backwards on the escalator, ragamuffins annoying the well-dressed shoppers. Jamie running through the aisles, out of control. Back to the first one again; she had never been that deprived or that lost!

She walked stiffly into the living area, the photos clutched in her hand. "What is this?"

John moved toward her. "What do you think you're doing in my files?"

"I was looking for Jamie's picture." Her lips felt frozen. "What is this?"

"Just some shots."

"You made me look like an—an urchin."

"That first shoot?" He smiled affectionately. "You were a little urchin then. . . ."

"No," she said. "No, I wasn't. I was somebody . . . I had a life plan . . . I was going to do things . . . I was . . ."

"Come on, Alice. It's just a photograph."

"And at the store . . . You egged him on, you had no right . . . He's very good for a little boy, he's *well*-mannered, you made us look like . . . like . . . There was lots more to us . . ." Tears were welling up. "Why?" she whispered.

"Alice, I never meant . . . I was just recording . . ."

"It's all lies! We weren't urchins!" She looked at him, bewildered, and then her face hardened with realization. "That project. It was part of that project you were working on, wasn't it?" She caught her breath. "Wasn't it?"

He took the photographs from her clenched fist. "I was going to tell you . . ." He put his arm around her. "I never meant to hurt you . . ."

"Jamie's a real person, really sweet and bright and special—" Her voice caught in a sob. "—and he's as good as *anybody*, and all you saw was just any old street kid. Your pictures are fakes, all of them! You had no right. . . ."

"Listen to me—"

"That's why you were always hanging around. You used me! You . . . You—" She punched him hard in the chest. "Worse than anyone!" She punched him again and felt his body register the impact. She was past caring about the tears wetting her cheeks, hurting her throat. "What were you hoping for?"

"Alice, stop."

"You were watching for me to crash, right? You were waiting around, hoping for the photo op when I crashed!" Her words were punctuated by hard automatic punches. "You never even saw me!" She sniffled and gasped. Her nose was running. "You manipulated and manipulated. . . ." Left fist, right fist, hard. She was dimly aware of his pained face and his rigid body accepting the blows. "I was *somebody*. I didn't need to be made over."

"Please . . . listen. . . ."

"Liar! Liar! I thought you *liked* me." She was washed with humiliation. Her face was wet and contorted. "You were so *nice* to Jamie."

"I did. I do."

She couldn't hold back the flood. "Where's your camera?" Punch. "How's this for a photo opportunity?" Punch. She was drenched in sorrow. Jamie!

"I wanted to help you. I want to help you now. Maybe at the very beginning, I . . ."

She stopped, exhausted, and her arms hung limply at her sides. "I don't need your help. You think you're so brilliant. You'll go to Japan or Belfast or wherever and set up the kids there the way you want and you won't see anything and it'll all be phony."

He looked stung. "You could be right. Maybe I've been in the fashion scene too long. . . ."

"You're always blaming the fashion scene. You're always knocking models. Well, you know something, Tanya and I put a lot into it. Those fur shots weren't all you."

237

"I know that, Alice. I was trying to warn you, protect you from—"

"*Protect* me! That shot in Kerstin's top—Lorline could use the moral turpitude clause. . . ."

"I doubt it. It's not something *Penthouse* would want, okay? I was doing a job, a serious photographic study of— There's not one picture there that's vulgar; some of your Mayhem stuff is more cause for embarrassment." He passed his hand over his brow. "Alice, trust my feeling for you. I never meant to hurt you. I want to be here for you now. . . ."

"Trust." She spit out the word.

"Yes, trust." He was angry and his hands gripped her shoulders. "All right, I'm sorry, I'm sorry! Maybe I made a mistake, but I'm not dishonorable!"

"Go to hell!"

"Alice. Alice, don't throw away everything between us."

"What? What's between us?"

He looked at her silently for a long time. Then he released her gently. "I'm going to take you back to the hospital."

"I don't need you!" She pushed him away with all her force and ran to the door. "I don't need anybody!" Except for a straggly-haired little boy.

27

A television screen was attached to the wall of the hospital lounge. The sound was turned off. A game show was in progress and frenetic contestants with orange faces gestured mutely.

On a couch underneath, a family sat huddled together, speaking in whispers.

Across the room, Claire and Alice sat stiffly, side by side, in hard-backed vinyl chairs.

"Waiting is the worst part," Claire said.

"No, it's not the worst part," Alice said.

On the screen, someone jumped up and down and applauded silently.

"The doctor said he'd be all right," Claire said. "Isn't that what he said?"

"No." Hadn't she understood between the lines? "The doctor said he'd be *physically* all right."

She could hear Claire draw in her breath.

"Maybe he was too young for a bike," Claire said.

"Kids have bikes," Alice said tonelessly. Her throat hurt. "He never had anything he wanted or needed or—"

"I didn't hear him leave. I guess the radio was on and—"

"If you'd just watched him better!"

"It wasn't my fault." Claire's voice broke. "It really wasn't."

There was a long silence, broken by the sound of sobbing from across the room. On the screen, cheese melted over a hamburger as French fries marched around the plate.

"I know. An accident," Alice finally mumbled, avoiding her eyes.

"I wasn't the worst mother, Alice. . . ."

"Ma, you don't have to—"

"I loved him and I did my best. I kept us together, no matter what, and it wasn't easy. I never abused or hit my kids and—"

Alice looked away. "I know that."

"And I never let anyone else, either. Remember when Jamie's father started throwing his weight around? I got rid of him, didn't I? I never punished Jamie or scared him. I was never anything like my folks."

"They punished you?" Alice looked up. Claire had always avoided talking about her family. It was as if they had never existed.

"I tried to make it nicer for my kids. You never had to run away."

"No. I never wanted to, Ma."

"Alice, I love him as much as you do." She became teary-eyed.

"I know you tried, Ma," she said.

"Oh, Alice. . . ."

Claire took her hand and gripped it tight. Alice loved her anyway, but there was no comfort in the warmth of her hand. Claire was Claire, incompetent as a mother; that's just the way it was. Whatever happened, whether Jamie came out of this whole or not, Alice would take charge. Real responsibility, Alice thought, not hit-or-miss, once-in-a-while. She'd never be a kid again. But, please God, help Jamie. . . .

A red, green, and yellow wheel rotated on the screen. The room smelled of plastic and dead air.

Then, over the intercom, "Lonner family, Intensive Care, third floor. Lonner family, Intensive—"

They jumped up, galvanized.

Alice was cold, ice cold hands and legs, as they rushed down the third floor corridor. She was dimly aware that John Alveira was there, a pained expression on his face. A nurse was saying "He's awake. You can see him, just for a moment."

Alice followed Claire into the room. There were other beds, separated by blue curtains. And then—Jamie. Alice slowly approached the bed on half-paralyzed legs. Fear had the taste of metal in her mouth.

"Baby, oh, baby!" Claire said, too loud.

"Jamie?" Alice whispered.

His eyes fixed on her and—oh God, thank you, God, they were bright and alive! She knew, she knew he was all right!

"Hi, Alice."

"Hi, Jamie." She could barely speak. Something like sunlight was flooding through her body.

"I didn't cry," he said. "I didn't know where I was and I was real scared, but I didn't cry."

"Oh, my baby," Claire sobbed.

"Do you know what happened to you? Do you know where you are now?" Alice asked.

"The nurse told me. Alice?"

"Yes, Jamie."

His voice dropped to a whisper. "The doctor is dumb. He asked me a lot of dumb questions. Like did I know my name and my birthday. Anybody would know that, right?"

"Right," Alice said.

"And two plus two. It was real dumb."

"It was," Alice agreed. She didn't know tears were running down her cheeks.

"How come you're crying? It was *my* accident and it's *my* head that hurts. . . . Right, Mommy?" His eyes sparkled with pride. Then, subdued, "Don't cry, Alice. Are you mad about the bike?"

"No. No, I'll never, ever be mad at you."

"You will, too. If I do something bad. . . . Alice, I was brave. I didn't cry."

They were shooed out of the room. John Alveira was standing awkwardly outside. "How is he?"

"He's—he's Jamie again!" Her face was shining. "He's okay. He's really okay!"

"That's great! That's wonderful!" John said. He moved toward her and for a moment she almost forgot, but then she backed away.

Alice visited Jamie in the hospital every day, in spite of Iris's complaints about missed bookings. Jamie was handling being away from home much better than she had expected. He was growing up, she thought, and somehow he seemed more confident. He loved the "magic motion" bed. He wasn't shy about asking the nurses for extra soda and ice cream; he found an aide to play Othello with him and he gloated about winning. Maybe a little extra attention was all that he had ever needed.

Outside, the limp mugginess of the city in summer was replaced by electric energy. The leaves of Central Park were turning color, framing the vitality of roller skaters and joggers and dogs romping on the lawn. Alice saw with sharpened vision everything that Jamie had almost missed.

It was strange to see kids on the streets carrying books and going back to school and not be among them. Then Jamie, too, went back to school—a small miracle with a brand-new lunch box. He could do anything or be anything; she wouldn't let that be wasted. No more waiting aimlessly for her to come home, no more dully watching TV for hours. She was making enough to put him in a good after-school program where he could learn to draw or sing or play ball or anything. Maybe she'd find a private school for him, with small classes, where he wouldn't get lost in the shuffle. . . .

Alice went back to work with cool professionalism. She knew how to find her best angle under the lights and how to project the mood that was wanted. She did her job and she no longer needed a steady stream of "You're beautiful . . . marvelous . . . wonderful . . . terrific." John had taught her well, she thought. John was gone now and she remembered him with less anger. He wasn't entirely to blame; she had thrown herself at him. God, how could the Mayhem hype have confused her into believing she was irresistible! Well, maybe her crush on that one unavailable man had protected her from being vulnerable to all those guys who collected models.

It was mostly an unglamorous job in glamorous costumes. Sometimes she laughed when everyone was up and the session became crazy-funny; often, she was bored and restless when she had to be immobile, pinned into place. "Exploit it," John had said, "don't *be* exploited." She knew she didn't want to do this forever. Whatever, she'd be more than a face; a mosquito bite would never become a personal tragedy. She might even ask Billie to block out one day a week and take some classes at the Art Students League, just for fun, just to see . . .

She made the arrangements with her private tutor in mid-September. He was a moonlighting assistant professor at New York University, quiet and bookish, but given to bursts of excitement when something piqued his interest.

"You have to tell me what you're looking for," he said. "Should I give you just enough to make it legal and pass the equivalency or do you want more depth?"

She hadn't thought about it. "Don't strain your brain, kiddo," John Alveira had said. "More depth," Alice told the tutor on the spur of the moment. "The works!"

When he heard she'd be going to Italy for the winter showings, he became enthusiastic and piled on the books and taught her about the Roman empire and the Renaissance, so she'd be aware of more than the drape of this year's skirts. There was some wonderful art in Florence, he said. Maybe she'd take a couple of days after the showings and just look around. . . .

And they talked a lot about history and different revolutions and wars. In high school, it had seemed like nothing but dry memorization of dates. Now, he was telling her a whole lot of interesting stories, with people believing in different things and winning and losing and passing things on to the next generation. She and Claire and Jamie were part of history, too! She knew there were answers for her somewhere; she had to learn enough to ask the right questions.

Modeling was buying her a custom-tailored private education, opportunity to travel, entree to all the pleasures of a great city, and she'd make the most of it. She could easily go on to college someday. . . . And if not, at least she was growing out of her ignorance. She was making herself over in more astounding ways than Damian, with all his skills, could have imagined.

Late in October, she received a letter from John Alveira. After a paragraph about the sights of Japan, it became more personal.

"For a lot of reasons, I was most comfortable in the role of detached observer. I don't think that was true anymore at the end of our time together. . . . The work has been going well. No more stereotypes and manipulation. Along with the pressure and burnout in the educational system here, there is discipline and pride and I think I've avoided slanting the story according to preconceived notions. It looks like there'll be a gallery exhibit and a book deal for the series (minus the Alice Lonner segment—that becomes part of my private archives of fond memories). On to Belfast in a while—and with a mind open to contradictions and surprises in that torn city. Thank you, Alice. . . . I hope you'll keep in touch. Eventually, I'll get back to the Big Apple. I've missed bagels, the *Times*, Ferrara's, and you—not quite in that order. . . ."

She could almost hear his voice as she read it. She could imagine his wry smile and his battered good looks. Her anger was dissolving. She'd write back to him. She was the same Alice Lonner, the basic Alice Lonner, no confusion, no airs, confident about where she was heading, and she wanted to let him know. "You're going to be one hell of a woman one day," John had said. Maybe he'd be around one day, to see. . . .

28

At the beginning of November, Alice was invited to Iris's country house again. A command performance. This time, she'd be one of the veteran Iris Martin girls.

Bambi was already in the limo when Kenneth pulled up in front of her building. Bambi, sleek and streamlined, whom she'd glimpsed so long ago in the agency reception room.

"How's it going, Alice?" Bambi said. "God, I hate these things. Who's going to be there?"

"Billie said Helaine from *Elegance Today!* and some designer, the guy that's doing triple crinolines—"

"Oh right, Jason Mercurio."

"I don't know who else. Oh, we're picking up a new girl Iris just signed."

"*Bor*-ing! We'll have to hear the complete Iris Martin speech. God, I wanted to *sleep* today!"

The car snaked through midtown traffic and headed up the West Side Drive. Bambi opened the partition to speak to Kenneth.

"Where are we going? Where does this chick live?"

"Washington Heights," Kenneth said. "Just a little detour."

"Washington Heights? Isn't that coke city?" Bambi said. "And speaking of coke, did you hear about Kerstin?"

Alice sat up straight in her seat. "What about Kerstin?"

"Iris dropped her."

"Iris dropped *Kerstin?*"

"Yes, I know. She was absolutely gorgeous, wasn't she? More so than any of us, to tell the truth. Iris kept her on as long as she possibly could."

"But why?"

"Come on, Alice, didn't you know? She was messed up on coke, messed up in a thousand ways, she was coming late for everything or not even showing. . . . Iris didn't have much choice."

"No, I didn't know," Alice said. She thought of Kerstin, giggling and generous. "I'm sorry. I liked her—I'm really sorry."

"Don't be *sorry* for her. She had everything going for her and she was just plain dumb. You know what I hear she's doing? Blue movies. I bet she's telling the folks back in Sweden she's a movie star."

"Denmark," Alice said.

"What?"

"She was from Denmark. A little town . . . a farm."

"Well, it's her own fault," Bambi said. "She could have had it all and she threw it away."

248

"She'd never even been in a big city before, I don't think. It must have been overwhelming," Alice said.

"Mmmm, I guess," Bambi said.

Kenneth pulled up in front of a five-story red brick building. Some men were washing a car at the curb; some little girls were playing hopscotch on the sidewalk, calling to each other in Spanish with high-pitched cries. An elderly woman sat on a stoop, holding a tired old dog on a leash. They all stared at the long, shiny limousine.

A tall thin girl came out of the doorway and Alice watched her as Kenneth held the car door open.

"Marisol Garcia?" he asked.

"Yes, I'm Marisol," she said in a shy wisp of a voice.

She looked frightened and she walked hesitantly, but somehow with a dancer's grace. She had huge, slanted hazel eyes, luminous and long-lashed under thick dark eyebrows. Her nose was delicate and classic, her mouth full, her cheekbones finely modeled under poreless skin. She had thick black hair, worn in one long braid down her back. Good for Laurent or Versace, Alice thought. Potentially a good exotic.

"Hi, I'm Alice and this is Bambi," Alice said.

"Oh, hi." Marisol sank down in the plush cushions. "A limo! I can't believe it! I'm so excited!" She nibbled at her lower lip. "Oh, I'm sorry. You're going to think I'm silly." She turned toward Alice. "Aren't you the Mayhem girl?"

"Yes, I—"

"The Mayhem girl! I can't believe I'm here. I should pinch myself."

"Hang on, kid, it's not all that great," Bambi drawled.

Alice looked at Marisol curiously. She was wearing a cheap

ice-cream pink windbreaker and a polyester skirt. Iris would do away with that soon. Her hands, under the pushed-up sleeves, were tapered and lovely.

"How did you get involved with Iris?" Alice asked.

"I sent my picture to the Iris Martin Agency, it was a good picture, my brother took it, and then I got a letter from Miss Martin and she said to see her if I ever came to New York." She spoke breathlessly, shyly, running her words together, words bursting out. "So I came and she gave me an appointment and then she signed me up. I'm staying at my mother's cousin's now, but it's too crowded and Miss Martin said I could stay with her, that's if it works out. Miss Martin is so wonderful!"

"How old are you?" Bambi said.

"Twelve."

"Twelve!"

"I know, I look much older 'cause I'm so tall, and Miss Martin said I'd be good for high fashion. I've already lost five pounds since last week! I'm so scared, though, I don't know how I'll work out, I'll die if I have to go back home. . . ."

The limousine whizzed by tenements and storefronts with signs in Spanish, past groups of teenagers lounging on the corners.

"You'll do well," Alice said. She felt suddenly tired and sad.

"It's like a dream come true 'cause that's all I've ever wanted, to be a model like—like the Mayhem girl. I'd see those commercials and pretend it was me, you know, in front of the bedroom mirror." She clapped a hand in front of her mouth.

"You'll think I'm silly. I can't believe I'm really in *New York* and sitting right next to you. In school, we had to do a composition on the woman we admired most in the world and I wrote the Mayhem girl."

Marisol had the right look for Mayhem, Alice thought. Maybe she shouldn't have asked Billie to block out one day a week, maybe it was a mistake. . . . Well, let Iris be annoyed! She'd ride it as long as she could, but she wouldn't build her world around it.

"The Mayhem girl," Alice said slowly, "is the hairdresser's skill and the makeup artist and good lighting and a terrific sound track and only a little bit of me." Marisol looked at her, dumbfounded. "I was lucky and so are you. It's the chance of a lifetime, if you use it for something, if you don't get stuck—" She saw Marisol's blank expression. My God, she was so impressed and so bewildered and *young!*

"If you ever need someone to talk to, if you need advice or . . . I'd be glad to . . ." Alice said.

"Oh, thanks. Miss Martin is giving me loads of advice about everything. She's like a mother!" Marisol smiled happily at Alice and there was nothing but dreams of glitter in her incredible eyes.

The car was on the West Side Drive again, passing the arc of the George Washington Bridge. The Palisades loomed across the river.

What could Alice possibly say that the girl could take in now? The high cheekbones could make her fantasies come true or leave her demolished. Marisol, she thought . . . good luck!